As Long As
Nothing Happens,
Nothing Will

As Long As
Nothing Happens,
Nothing Will

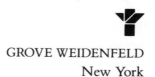 Zhang Jie

Translated from the Chinese
by Gladys Yang, Deborah J. Leonard
and Zhang Andong

GROVE WEIDENFELD
New York

Published by Grove Weidenfeld
A division of Grove Press, Inc.
841 Broadway
New York, NY 10003–4793

First published in Great Britain in 1988 by
Virago Press Inc.

Library of Congress Cataloging-in-Publication Data

Chang, Chieh, 1937–
    [Short stories.   English]
    As long as nothing happens, nothing will : stories / by Zhang Jie ;
[translated from the Chinese by Gladys Yang, Deborah J. Leonard,
and Zhang Andong]. — 1st ed.
        p.   cm.
    Reprint. Originally published : London : Virago, 1988.
    Contents : What's wrong with him? — Professor Meng abroad —
The other world — Something else? — Today's agenda.
    ISBN 0-8021-1144-0 (alk. paper)
    1. Chang, Chieh, 1937–   —Translations, English.   I. Title.
PL2837.C486A287   1991
895.1'35—dc20   91-378
                                                                     CIP

Manufactured in the United States of America

Printed on acid-free paper

Designed by Joyce Weston

First American Edition 1991

10   9   8   7   6   5   4   3   2   1

As Long As
Nothing Happens,
Nothing Will

⌖ The Other World

IN a small town, the county seat of a very poor county, remote from any city, a famous man appeared. He emerged suddenly, surprising the local people as much as if a golden ear of corn had sprung overnight from the land. They were astonished, bewildered and envious.

Just two weeks before, Rong Chang Lan was an unknown fine-arts teacher in the county's middle school. He had a very short, flat haircut, thick lips, small, heavy-lidded eyes and a well-made, powerful body. He wore a black cotton jacket that buttoned down the center, blue polyester slacks and green army-surplus sneakers. If you stood him among the local youths, he would be absolutely indistinguishable from them.

But if you entered his room you would see countless tubes of oil paints, brushes and more brushes, and landscape paintings hanging on and leaning against the walls.

The paintings were nothing special. A small river, an ancient pagoda, a few crooked old trees, that temple halfway up the hill. It was a sin. The people worked so hard to produce and process the cotton, it was spun and woven with such pains, only to be so carelessly covered with paint. They themselves begrudged even the cloth they used to make their clothes.

His paintings were far less popular than the gauche New Year's posters sold at the Xinhua bookshops. On one poster a woman agronomist is seen explaining how to use a new, improved kind of cotton seed; on another a fat baby holds a huge goldfish in his arms; on yet another, a mother-in-law and her son's wife live happily together. . . .

The people simply shook their heads when they looked at Rong's paintings. Humph . . . to think he graduated from the university of this province!

It took the head of the Bureau of Culture and Education a long time to think of a good job to offer Rong Chang Lan after his graduation. What was the best job for him? Headmaster? He was not a member of the Party or the Youth League. Teacher? The salary he'd begin receiving upon graduation would be almost the same as that of a headmaster. Dean? No, he was much too gullible and slow-witted for such a position. When he was asked what sort of job he'd prefer, his answer was simple. He eagerly wanted to be a middle school fine-arts teacher.

He was like a shriveled grain of corn, planted in the earth, motionless for years, that suddenly sprouted and grew.

Nobody knew who had taken those paintings to the capital city of the province and put them on exhibition. Nobody knew how or why the foreigner took a fancy to the painting of that half-ruined pagoda and paid two thousand yuan on the spot for it.

Two thousand yuan! That was enough money for a

peasant to build a two-story house! People stood in front of the image of the ruined pagoda and wondered how it could be worth two thousand yuan to anyone.

Very soon after that came word from the provincial government telling Rong to come immediately to the capital to meet a foreigner.

A teacher of fine arts going to meet a foreigner. That had to mean he was important, didn't it?

Rong Chang Lan had not been on a train for years; he found it much more crowded than before. There were three people packed into seats designed for two. And it was even worse in the aisles—people stood and sat in every possible and impossible space. Rong understood when the attendant could not serve the boiled water and food on time. He thoughtfully chewed the dry steamed bread he had brought with him, using his tongue and the little saliva in his mouth to turn, soak and soften it, and his teeth to flatten it enough to get it down his esophagus. He was lost in thoughts about the complicated and hectic world he would soon enter.

His imagination and hopes had been awakened by the notice he'd received telling him that a foreigner wanted to buy his painting. Until now his life had been peaceful and routine; he had been like a bush in a wide, open field with plenty of space around him. His life, which had run parallel to that other world, was now going to intersect with it. Could he handle it? He'd never thought about it before.

He had been on the train for several hours, unaware of the changing landscape until the voice on the loudspeaker began to describe the scenery of the provincial capital as though reciting a poem. Rong Chang Lan was suddenly aware that he was in G City.

He stretched and flexed his legs, numb from hours of standing. He picked up his green canvas bag with an old-style airplane printed on the side. He patiently followed the crowd of people inching their way toward the exit.

Rong was transfixed for some minutes as he stood in the middle of the large square outside the railway station. There seemed to be so much of everything: so many big buildings, so many cars, so many people, so many shops . . . and so many foreign tourists dressed in so many bright colors. A short time before, the voice on the loud-speaker had explained that there was a famous mountain and a hot spring not far from G City. He hadn't known that when he was a student here.

To Rong Chang Lan's surprise a taxi appeared. A man waved his hand and at this signal the taxi responded quickly and slid smoothly to a stop. The man and the people with him got into the comfortable car as unhur-riedly and naturally as they would have gotten on a bus.

Rong Chang Lan took a deep breath, as though he was about to dive into the depths of this prosperous city in order to understand it more deeply. Then he began to look for a hotel.

AT midnight he was awakened from a deep sleep. He got up from his short, narrow iron bed, which had been installed in what during the day was a public bathhouse. This was the cheapest sort of accommodation he could find. Half awake, he looked at the line of small iron beds, each bearing a sleeping body in some position of repose.

He heard the thin and thick sounds of snoring coming from many throats and felt as if he were in an *arhat* temple.

"Are you Comrade Rong Chang Lan?" Two men in their thirties wearing blue serge Mao jackets bowed to him.

"Yes." Rong looked at these two complete strangers who for some reason seemed eager to find him.

"What a joker you are, hiding yourself here. You made us work pretty hard. First we made a long-distance call to the government offices where you live and they told us you had gotten on the train. We put up a large board in the square outside the train station that said 'Comrade Rong Chang Lan, please meet your party here.' . . . You didn't see it?" the slightly younger of the two asked.

"No, I didn't see it—I'm sorry." Rong had not expected that anyone would meet him at the train station, so he hadn't even noticed that there was any such board. But he was too moved to say anything.

"We checked every hotel, big and small, in G City, and finally we've found you here. Let's go. We've already arranged a more suitable place for you to stay. But we're very sorry to have awakened you from your sleep," said the older man.

"Is it all right if I just stay here? This place is fine."

"It would be more convenient for us to contact you at the place we've arranged. Let's go." Saying this, he courteously picked up Rong's green canvas bag.

"Let me carry that—let me carry that." Rong tried to take his bag from the man.

"No, I'll carry it—I'll carry it." The two men quickly went ahead to lead the way.

"Why does the public bathhouse always have to smell of dirty feet?" sniffed the younger man to his partner.

"Don't you remember what I told you—you needn't worry that you'll be taken for a mute if you keep your mouth shut more often. Do you want to be relieved of your duties?"

>< 2

Rong Chang Lan tightly rolled up the small jacket he had taken off. He took an old newspaper from under the teapot and wrapped it around the jacket. Then he tied the roll tightly with string and put it into the cupboard. He closed the cupboard door and raised his head to look at himself in the mirror. Seeing himself in the gray polyester Western-style suit, he wondered whether he looked handsome or ugly.

He recalled the embarrassing situation of the evening before, when the hotel guard had stopped him at the hotel gate. In reality, what did it matter what he wore— surely the fact of his small jacket would not prevent people acknowledging him as the artist who'd painted the ruined pagoda?

Yet many things conspired to make him take off his small jacket and put on the gray suit: the resplendent hotel lobby; the shiny marble floors and the pillars that reflected like mirrors; the dark red carpet; the crystal chandeliers; the silk bedspreads; the petal-shaped lamps mounted on the walls; the bathtub, commode and telephone, all in shades of pale yellow; the perfumed foreigners in the elevator; and the very polite dining room attendants who wore uniforms much more dignified than his clothes.

The matter of the small jacket and the polyester Western suit annoyed him. Which meant more—the painting of the ruined pagoda or the polyester suit?

He didn't know when he'd started to think continually about his painting of the pagoda—as if he was putting its meaning, its very existence to the test.

The writer had said, "To tell you the truth, the works themselves are secondary; the key point is public relations. Do you know Ke Yi Yun?" He mentioned the name of a person of authority in provincial fine-arts circles. He said the name as if he were naming a weapon with great deterrent capabilities.

"No, I don't."

"You don't?" The writer gave him an astonished look. "You have to get to know him if you want to get a foot into this territory." He explained all this to Rong as if talking to a person who had lost his way. He received no response from Rong, but he continued anyway. "The literary giants like Shakespeare relied on the nobility; artists from ancient times to today, and in foreign countries as well as our own, have all lived in this way. Without strong backing, you don't stand a chance."

That morning, Rong had been awakened by the writer's knock at his door. And before Rong had had a chance to ask who was there, the writer had let himself in.

"I'm Wu Zhi Heng," he had said with absolute self-confidence, which suggested he believed his name was known around the world. But when he saw that Rong appeared to have no idea who Wu Zhi Heng was, Wu waved his hand in a magnanimous way, adding simply, "I'm a writer," and sat down on the sofa. He didn't name any books or articles he had written. It would have been pointless to name them for this ignorant and ill-informed country bumpkin.

"Get dressed and we'll have breakfast together." When he saw Rong Chang Lan hesitate, he said in a way that was half appreciative, half cursing, "The tempo of life has been hopelessly quickened; we get to know people and we forget them in the wink of an eye."

Facing this stranger who behaved like an old friend at their first meeting, Rong had begun to dress. As soon as he stretched his naked legs out from under the blanket, Wu said, "You ought to buy yourself some pajamas."

Rong hurried into his trousers, ashamed of his hairy legs. But in his haste he put his trousers on backward and found his fly at the back when he pulled them up to his waist.

Wu had turned a blind eye to him and said, "Remember, I am the first writer who wanted to write a novel using you as a model. So please don't give interviews to any other writers."

"Write about me? No—no, there's nothing to write about me." Rong Chang Lan had held his small jacket in his arms and was so surprised and confused he dropped heavily onto the bed. For generations his family had been ordinary people, completely unknown to the world; they had lived quietly and obscurely. How could they suddenly become characters in a novel? Was this a blessing or a curse?

"Don't be nervous. I won't write about you by name,

but just take you as my prototype. Just as you need a
model when you paint. Novels are both true and false. As
Cao Xueqin said in his classic novel *The Story of the
Stone*,★ 'All the pages were full of impossible words.'
They make the true false and the false true. What are you
afraid of? . . . Ah, don't just sit there; hurry up and get
dressed or it'll be too late to get breakfast." As he said
this, Wu Zhi Heng had looked down at his new leather
shoes. The toes were quite long, and on the outer side of
each was an ornamental metal button. The heels were
high, almost like high heels on women's shoes. He noticed a scuff mark on the toe of one shoe and went into the
bathroom to get some toilet paper to clean it. "So, I have
to live with you for a few days. Just as Chairman Mao
said, 'Eat together, live together, labor together with
workers, peasants and soldiers.' I must do this to get to
know you better. But 'live together'—not necessary.
When they are asleep, the great and the lowly are almost
equal, I'm afraid. And 'labor together'—probably also
unnecessary. Even though we both play with pens and
brushes, we do different work and it's impossible to do it
together. I've seen your painting. If you play your cards
right . . ." Wu had paused here, wondering whether to
speak the rest of his thought. He had looked at the tall,
strong man before him and felt small and weak as a
child—damn it. Perhaps it was the appeal of Rong's
paintings that had made him involuntarily honest with
him. "If you play your cards right, you could very
quickly become popular and successful."

★ *Translators' note:* Written around 1760 and also known as *The Dream of the Red
Chamber*, this is the great novel of manners of Chinese literature.

"Popular and successful?" Rong Chang Lan had re-peated Wu's words. What did these words have to do with him? He wasn't a film star or a pop singer.

"Yes, 'popular and successful'—do you object to those words? Those words could describe you. You'll see."

Rong turned away from the mirror; he had to hurry to the dining room downstairs. The writer who had the task of "eating together" with him was waiting there. He opened the door and went out of the room feeling con-strained. He assumed that the whole world would re-member him running around in a small jacket only the day before and that everyone would be surprised by his sudden change. Yet no one gave his polyester Western suit a second look. The world went on just as it had before he wore this suit.

While Rong waited for the elevator near the ninth-floor service desk, he noticed a man with very thickly greased hair, wearing a dark Western suit. The man was explain-ing how his camera worked to the girl behind the counter. At first glance the suit looked all right, but upon closer examination it was very strange: it wasn't long enough where it ought to be long and wasn't short enough where it ought to be short; it wasn't fitted enough where it ought to be fitted and wasn't loose enough where it ought to be loose.

He said to the girl behind the counter, "We call this kind of camera a 'fool's camera.' The camera automat-ically sets the focus and exposure. You merely push this button. Let me take your picture?"

"No, thanks," she said.

"It's color film."

"No, it's really not necessary."

"I will leave for Beijing tomorrow, then fly to Germany. Germany is a good place. You must go to Europe if you ever go abroad. There's nothing interesting anywhere else."

"Have you been to Germany before?"

"Ah . . . no . . ."

"Do you often visit foreign countries?"

"Ah . . . we have, ah . . . many opportunities to visit foreign countries in our office." After saying this, he turned from the counter, walked over to the elevator and pushed the up button. But Rong had already pushed the down button. He wondered which way the elevator would go.

It stopped at the ninth floor. Rong hesitated, then entered; the doors closed and the elevator began to move. It stopped on the first floor. He left the elevator with an apologetic look at the other man, but to his surprise the man followed him, striding comfortably into the lobby.

Hadn't he wanted to go up? Perhaps he wasn't much better at all this than Rong Chang Lan and didn't know how to push the right button for up or down. But obviously he had more courage than Rong. No matter which button you pushed, you'd be right fifty percent of the time. Nobody would notice which direction you were going except someone like Rong Chang Lan.

An English-speaking woman in her fifties stopped Rong as he was going through the lobby.

"Excuse me, sir. Would you please take my bags to room nine-twelve?" She smiled in a noble way. Her lips, which were colored by lipstick, curved beautifully. Her gray hair was pinned up. She wore a loose gray flannel dress and dark red suede ankle boots. She was very pleasant to look at. She obviously mistook him for an attendant. No doubt it was because the color of his Western suit was very close to that of the hotel workers' uniforms.

He turned his head and searched but couldn't find even the shadow of an attendant. She stood smiling and waiting. So he bent and picked up her two large suitcases.

What a coincidence—her room was just opposite his.

"Thanks; here's your tip."

He smiled, shook his head and backed out of the room.

THE two empty beer cans on the dining room table indicated that the writer had been waiting for a long time. Because of this, he looked at Rong's suit hypercritically. "Why didn't you buy a pure-wool Western suit—didn't you want to spend the money?"

"It wasn't necessary. What would I do with a pure-wool Western suit when I return to my village? This suit is good enough for this occasion."

"Are you really planning to go back to the country?"

"Yes, I really am."

"Don't you want to work in G City?"

"No, I don't. At least, I never thought about it before this very second."

"How about now?"

"I don't know yet."

Wu Zhi Heng passed him the menu. "Let's order some food."

Rong Chang Lan read the menu line by line, from the cold dishes, seafood, chicken, duck, eggs, meat, soups and vegetables to the dessert. He was the host, so he must act like a host. But not only was the menu difficult to understand, it dazzled him. He didn't know what all the dishes tasted like, much less understand their names, except for braised prawns and sliced chicken in egg-white sauce, which the writer had ordered at noon. "You order, please—order anything you like," Rong said.

Wu muttered to himself for a moment, then named the dishes they would have: sea cucumber and pigs' feet; black carp in oil, green cabbage with mushrooms. "Ordering dishes is a kind of knowledge, but it's easy to learn. It's knowledge you can obtain if you spend money." He smiled without showing his teeth.

Just then, a small, tidily dressed old man entered the dining room with a woman whose hair was disheveled. They walked directly to a table that seemed to be perpetually reserved for them.

"Do you see them? That's the famous calligrapher X and the famous woman writer Y."

The famous woman writer had a very artistic, bohemian style about her. She wore a pair of black cloth shoes—wore them like slippers, her feet thrust in and the backs flattened down by her heels. Her white nylon socks were very stained. The fourth button of her coffee-colored wool cardigan was buttoned into the fifth buttonhole. An excess length of belt lapped down below her cardigan. Her getup was hardly more elegant than Rong's small jacket, but the waiters all served her very respectfully.

"These are important guests of the hotel. They stay here for months at a time—eat free, drink free and live free."

"Why does the hotel put out so much money on them?"

"The hotel isn't losing money; the old master does

calligraphy for the hotel. Foreigners, especially Japanese, like his work very much. A scroll can be sold for one thousand yuan. See that wooden plaque on the wall? That's a masterpiece by this *xian sheng.*★ It's very valuable, you know. And the writer writes advertising copy for the hotel. Under her pen everything blossoms. She can even write a beautiful essay on toads if you ask her, so you can imagine how much more she can accomplish with a sumptuous hotel. After you become famous, you can paint several paintings for this hotel and they will feed you generously as well."

"Then why don't you write something for this hotel?"

"Me? To tell you the truth, I have written something for them. If I hadn't, how do you suppose I could have been so familiar with their menu? I am familiar with more than just the menu here. . . . Do you see that older woman over there?"

Rong followed Wu's eyes and found a very beautiful, elegantly dressed woman sitting and calmly watching a waiter serve her. She didn't lift a finger to move a chopstick or a dish, just let the waiter support his heavy tray loaded with soup with one hand and with the other rearrange saucers, large plates, and large and small bowls to make room on the table for the heavy soup bowl. She must be accustomed to being served. How could she eat so much food, anyway?

"She is Mrs. B."

Rong knew without asking that she must be a very important person, just by looking at Wu's face.

"And over there, the young man in the silver-gray

★ *Translators' note:* A reverential form of address.

jacket and gold-framed glasses is Ke Yi Yun's son. He formerly studied novel writing under me but now studies painting with Yi Yang. Painting is more profitable than novel writing: you have money if you want money; you have status if you want status; you have a house if you want a house. You are welcomed wherever you go. Anyone with even a little education knows he should collect a piece or two by a famous painter. To put it more pleasantly, it's a sign of refinement. And of course, a painting never goes down in value. Who, on the other hand, needs a writer? If he becomes famous and earns money he's the only one who profits, not the person who buys his work. If he goes so far as to give a book to someone, it's pointless—even his signature is worthless. Would our one billion people be any worse off if there wasn't even a single writer or book in existence? No, the machines in the factories would still produce their goods, and rice would still grow in the fields."

The dishes were served and the waiter asked, "Would you like rice?"

Wu surveyed the dishes on the table and said, "I don't want any, how about you?"

"Yes, I'd like some," said Rong. He was unaccustomed to this way of eating. No matter how many dishes he ate, he never felt satisfied unless he ate rice at the end of his meal.

Wu poured a glass of beer for Rong and said, "Come on, please don't stand on ceremony, eat!" He said it as if he were the host. He raised his own chopsticks with the air of someone prepared to shoulder a responsibility, picked up a large piece of sea cucumber and put it into his mouth. He was very skillful with his chopsticks. He could pick up even the slipperiest things with ease. But Rong had no such skill. He tried several times, but the sea cucumber kept slipping from between his chopsticks. He had to use the spoon and attack it from both sides, at last trapping that elusive morsel. But before he could get it into his mouth, the sea cucumber leaped through the gap between the spoon and chopsticks, falling into his bowl. The sauce that coated it splashed and he felt a hot splotch on his cheek. He wiped his hand across it and knew that the sauce had splashed onto his face.

". . . Writing a book is much harder than painting a painting; a writer really works his heart out when he writes. You simply sweep your brush whenever you feel like it, and you earn thousands of yuan in one day! But how about us? We write painstakingly for months and earn no more than a few hundred yuan. And if we say the wrong thing, we get in trouble. It's no use trying to explain that you didn't mean to say anything objectionable, because people are sure you did. In fact, I'm not as talented as other people." He stuck out his thumb and gestured toward the woman writer, who sat with her head lowered, chewing busily. "But I need to hold my own, even in this field, don't I? To do that, you know, I have to pay a lot of attention to cultivating public relations. Nobody would notice my work if I didn't. A few hundred yuan doesn't go very far." As he spoke, the look of self-confidence and self-satisfaction vanished from his face.

"Then why did you decide to be a writer?"

"That's a very complicated question. Look." He took a coin from his pocket and laid it on the table. "See this coin? On one side is the national emblem." He pointed to one side of the coin. Turning it over, he said, "And on this side are engraved the characters for two fen." Together they stared at the coin in silence. The coin reflected the weak light coming from the orange lamp of the dining room.

✄ 3

It was a truly astonishing meeting. The person who had traveled from Beijing especially to meet Rong was the woman who lived across the hall, the same one who had mistaken him for a hotel porter.

"Hello, sir . . . I . . . I'm very sorry . . . uh, please forgive me for making such a rude mistake." Mrs. Hassen, obviously embarrassed, nervously clasped and unclasped her hands as she spoke.

"Never mind. I was very happy to be able to help you." After Mrs. Hassen had taken him for a porter, several other people had made the same mistake. He never refused or explained when anyone stopped him to ask for directions or assistance.

"Do you two already know each other?" A series of questions raced through the minds of the escorts. How and where did these two meet? What did the words "rude mistake" mean? And what constituted the "help" that Rong had given Mrs. Hassen?

"Oh, yes." Again Mrs. Hassen smiled her gracious smile.

"We've barely met," said Rong.

Their contrasting and vague responses heightened the curiosity of the escorts. Rong saw them exchange sly, wondering glances. One of them quickly recorded the dialogue in his notebook when no one was looking.

"Can you speak French?" asked Mrs. Hassen.

"No." Rong had studied English when he was at the university.

"How about English?"

"A little."

"Very good." Mrs. Hassen rested her folded hands on her knees, which were pressed tightly together, and said calmly, "My husband came here on business from Beijing one month ago, just at the time your exhibition was on. He brought back one of your paintings and it charmed me. . . . Now I've come here especially to see your other works. I hope to get to know you and to explain my husband's idea for our company to bring you to our country for one year to lecture, exchange ideas and exhibit your work. The exact time will be up to you. I hope you won't refuse."

"Ah, this . . ." Rong Chang Lan was completely unprepared for a conversation that came to the point so entirely without preliminaries. He had never had contact with a foreigner before and had never been taught how to manage such a conversation. He knew from *The History of the World's Fine Arts* that the galleries and museums in Mrs. Hassen's country were the ones all of the world's artists longed to see. Artists felt they could die happy if they'd had the chance to view and study the art in those collections. One could wait a lifetime and never have this sort of opportunity. There was no doubt about it—it would be very helpful and enlightening for his future work. He had never even dreamed of such a chance before. It was like a colorful cloud in the sky. But now it had descended and settled over him so easily that he could hardly believe it was real.

───────

Mrs. Hassen waited for his response.

"Thanks. Thank you for your kindness."

Mrs. Hassen nodded silently. She then turned the conversation to painting. She was alert and resourceful. She seemed to know a great deal about painting.

"Do you paint?" asked Rong.

"No, I don't paint, but I study," she said.

The conversation ranged deep and wide. The interpreter grew tired and the escorts were tired too. They struggled to stifle their yawns, and one of them peeked repeatedly at his watch.

Mrs. Hassen didn't miss any of this, in spite of her involvement in the conversation. But she had obtained the necessary permission and spent good money on travel and lodging, so she was determined to finish the job properly. She didn't stop until she felt the conversation was finished. She caught the eye of the escort who was looking at his watch again and said, "Thank you. I don't have any more questions."

Mrs. Hassen gave a banquet at the hotel to honor the leaders and important figures in the art world of G City. In reality, the banquet was for Rong Chang Lan. On the basis of her experience, she judged that Rong was an artist well on his way to his best work. But he was still an innocent babe in the world of public relations. She very much wanted to help him. The morning meeting had not satisfied her very much—she hadn't expected this sort of half-official meeting. She wanted to have a free conversation with him alone next time. It was convenient that their rooms were near each other.

Rong was introduced for the first time to the leader of the G City Artists' Association, whose name, Ke Yi Yun, carried such power that it crashed like thunder in the ears of the city's artists. Rong probably wouldn't have had such an honor if he had not been seated on Mrs. Hassen's left while Comrade Ke was seated on her right.

"Mm—good," said Comrade Ke. He extended his large, fat hand, letting Rong Chang Lan shake it for a second, then quickly withdrew it. He didn't even glance at Rong; he was busy. There were so many people clustering around him, asking his opinion of their works. He was fat and a little short of breath. He remained seated so that people could take turns standing beside him to ask their questions.

These people talked of many things. Comrade Ke said to whomever he was speaking to, regardless of the topic, "Mm—good." The words were brief and their meaning was vague. Comrade Ke was still saying "Mm—good" when Mrs. Hassen proposed a toast and thanked everyone for coming to her banquet. Comrade Ke said only, "Mm—good."

Mrs. Hassen thought it strange that Rong Chang Lan didn't drink even a drop of wine. "No, beer is fine."

"Oh. Well then, do you smoke?"

"No."

"Most unusual for an artist, but all the better, and your paintings have an otherworldly feeling about them. You have a very bright future before you. . . . What do you think, Comrade Ke?"

"Mm—good," said Comrade Ke.

The conversation between Mrs. Hassen and Comrade Ke spread around the room like the aroma of mellow wine. People who had previously ignored him began to regard Rong Chang Lan with some interest. They supposed that his gray Western suit wasn't that bad—the artist shouldn't be too clothes conscious, too aware of his appearance. After all, artists were different from movie stars. It was difficult to read the thoughts expressed by the small eyes hidden behind their thick eyelids; the thick, protruding lips suggested the self-willed character of the artist. . . . The people appraised him volubly within his hearing, without any hesitation, as if he were an insensible piece of beefsteak on their plate.

After they had reached a consensus and decided that nothing would be lost by acknowledging his existence, the people smiled at Rong Chang Lan.

After the banquet had ended, Mrs. Hassen said to Comrade Ke, "Mr. Ke, I hope to have a chance to discuss with you the arrangements for Mr. Rong's visit to my country."

Ke Yi Yun stopped in his tracks, tapped the carpet with his cane, thought for a while and said, "What you suggest is very significant. . . . What we have done in this regard in the past has not been enough. . . . We must do more in the future to enrich our understanding and to promote the development and prosperity of culture." Comrade Ke spoke the predictable and empty formulas expected from officials.

"I will wait for you to set up an appointment with me."

"Mm—good." Comrade Ke panted slightly and, using his cane, walked out of the room surrounded by people.

I T was only early spring, but he was sweating so heavily that he smelled—it was as if he had been hoeing in the fields all day, instead of meeting and talking with that assortment of VIPs. Rong Chang Lan jumped into the bathtub as soon as he returned to his room. He scrubbed his body with his hands, using plenty of soap to clean himself from head to foot. At this moment the telephone rang sharply. He stood up in the tub, dripping with soap and water, not knowing quite what to do. Even though he was alone in the room and the door was locked, he couldn't bring himself to answer the phone naked.

The phone continued to ring, and began to sound urgent, as if it really wanted him to answer. He had just gathered up his courage when he realized that there was a phone on the bathroom wall, an extension of the main telephone.

He picked up the receiver at once; Mrs. Hassen said, "Hello, Mr. Rong, were you in bed?"

"No."

"May I come over and talk with you?"

He wasn't sure whether it was suitable or not. It was at least nine-thirty.

"Sorry, maybe I've interrupted your rest."

"Oh, no, no, please do come—in about ten minutes." Rong hurriedly rinsed the soapsuds from his body and got dressed. He sat on the sofa waiting for Mrs. Hassen, his mind in turmoil. In precisely ten minutes, no more and no less, there was a knock on the door. He suddenly realized what a mess the whole room was, but there was no time now to straighten it.

"I just couldn't rest until I had a talk with you. Do you mind if I smoke?"

"No, please make yourself comfortable."

She lit a long, thin cigarette and drew on it in a leisurely manner. She sat there looking straight at Rong, ignoring the rest of the room. He felt as if a heavy load had been taken from his shoulders. "I have been to see your paintings. They were displayed in the remotest corner of the exhibition hall. I think I should tell you that not many people see them where they are; people are only interested in seeing the more prominently displayed popular art. Were you aware of this?"

"Not until this moment." Rong had never been to see his own works exhibited—he didn't dare to. He had not attended the exhibition's opening ceremonies, either. He had entrusted all the arrangements to his teacher and classmates. After all, what qualified him to stand at the entrance of the exhibition hall like the older, well-established artists, to welcome all those VIPs? And there was no guarantee that there would be even ten people who would come to see an unknown artist's first show. People would be skeptical of that simple and rather crude invitation card; they would ask, "Who is Rong Chang Lan? Why haven't I ever heard of him before? What has he painted?"

"Does this bother you?"

"Of course." He felt as if he had been hit in the chest by a brick, but he quickly freed himself from the feeling. "My aim is to express what I feel. If people don't want to accept what I have to say, I can't force them to."

"But is it rewarding for you this way? Your work can only really have value after it has been recognized by society."

"What you say isn't quite correct. It may take time

before I am accepted—some artists are recognized only after their death."

"Why should you have to wait that long? You'll never have the satisfaction of knowing you're accepted."

"The people will know it."

There was a knock at the door.

"Come in!" Rong thought it strange that someone would visit him at this hour.

A room attendant opened the door a crack, stuck in his head and said, "Wouldn't you like some boiled water?"

"No, not right now. I did want some this morning but didn't have any."

"Sorry." The attendant closed the door and went away.

"But I believe these paintings can be understood and accepted now, in the West," Mrs. Hassen said. "There are no national boundaries between the arts."

"But paintings are saturated with the soul and spirit of their own country. I don't know what to call it—traditional ideology? Culture and art contain the crystallization of the wisdom of mankind. And each nation's art contains characteristics of that nation. You have said that there's an 'otherworldly feeling' about my paintings; it's difficult for me to know where it comes from. For example, the painting Mr. Hassen bought. How could I have conveyed the 'otherworldly feeling' that you describe if I had not heard countless stories about pagodas since I was a little boy? There must be a story hidden in nearly every pagoda here. If I hadn't stood at the foot of that pagoda and heard the calls of the birds that live in it, if I hadn't watched the grass on the ruined wall of the pagoda turn green in the spring and yellow in the autumn, if I hadn't seen the pagoda gradually crumbling and eroding under the blowing winds and the beating rains, I never could have created that feeling. An artist would be merely a technician if he lost his soul." Rong had never said so much to a stranger before. He felt quite odd—where had the words come from?

Mrs. Hassen listened intently. "I think you're right, but I still feel sorry for you."

Another knock at the door.

"Come in!"

It was the same room attendant. He edged through the door sideways. "I'm here to clean the room."

Mrs. Hassen stood up. "I think I'll say good-bye now. If I stay any longer, this gentleman will find it difficult to come up with another excuse to come into your room. I don't want to make him uncomfortable. Good night."

"Good night."

Rong Chang Lan was embarrassed and angry; he could feel the blood rushing to his face. He wouldn't grumble at the attendant—that would only make him sound guilty, like a thief who had been caught. What's more, did he have any good reason to accuse the attendant? He hadn't been impolite. Actually, one should probably admire his good service.

No doubt the attendant thought that a foreign woman and a Chinese man alone in a room together at such an hour must be up to no good. He tried to put them into an ambiguous situation. Rong felt he owed Mrs. Hassen an apology, although it had not been his fault. How obliviously insulting these people could be to others! Hypocritical capitalists would simply plant a listening device or a camera somewhere in the room. They would secretly hold you in their hands while outwardly showing you

endless respect. The attendant unnecessarily rearranged
several objects on the desk and gave a few swipes with a
cloth to the bathtub. He left quietly.

Rong Chang Lan locked his door, even fastened the
security chain, and went to bed. He was very sleepy.
He expected to fall asleep quickly, but he couldn't. He
had insomnia. His mind spun this way and that, like a
weather vane in the wind. Why had he fastened both
locks on his door, like a frightened, overwrought old
woman? He suddenly felt foolish. What did he fear? Did
he hope to lock out that world outside his door? If that
was what he really wanted, why had he been so filled
with hope and imagination when he'd had the chance to
come here? His village was humble and remote, but people there were not competitive and life was peaceful. Like
a moth drawn to a flame, he had been drawn to G City.

✼ 4

The desk clerk in the lobby said to the seventh group of
guests who had come wanting to see Rong Chang Lan,
"I'm sorry, but no one answers the phone in room nine-
oh-nine."

The guests sat patiently on the sofa near the reception
desk. A man who seemed to know everything said to
several young coquettish women seated around him,
"Mrs. Hassen is famous for collecting the works of well-
known artists. Her words carry a lot of weight in the
West. Rong Chang Lan will soon be world famous if he
earns her good opinion. When he goes abroad he will be
treated very well. It will be a very rich harvest for him—
both in financial terms and in terms of his reputation."

"Ah . . ." the young women sighed enchantedly. They drew closer to the man who knew everything, every fiber straining to catch each word he said. He stuttered a little, and they anxiously watched his mouth. They would have reached in with their hands to extract all he knew about Rong Chang Lan had it been possible.

"Is he married?" asked a young woman who was so nervous that her throat felt tight.

"No. But I believe he will have a peach-blossom fate, a romance, very soon," said a bald man who always had beautiful women around him.

"If someone became his wife, could she go abroad with him?" asked a woman wearing a silk jacket.

"Of course. Don't you read the newspaper? Now the famous writers and artists always take their wives or husbands when they go abroad."

"Ah . . ." The same woman pressed her hands together before her and sighed a sigh that held all her hopes. She looked at her watch and said, "My goodness, when can we see him? We've waited for an hour and a half already. Where could he have gone?" Those were the words she spoke, but in her mind she was hoping that at that very moment no other woman was stealing him from her.

Just then a distinguished-looking man walked up to the reception desk with an equally distinguished-looking woman. "I'm here to see Rong Chang Lan in room nine-oh-nine."

The man who knew everything told his entourage, "That's the famous painter Yi Yang. He has friends in very high places."

This news caused a sensation among the young women. "Some say he's envious of talented people and is arrogant and haughty, but these seem to be rumors. Look, hasn't he come to see Rong Chang Lan? This is the behavior of a master artist."

"Who is the woman with him?"

"The daughter of the head of the Bureau of Culture."

Clearly, Yi Yang came often to this hotel. The clerk treated him with special solicitude. "How do you do? . . . He seems to be absent from his room right now. We have called several times, but there's no answer."

"Would you try again?"

At last Rong was awakened by the ringing phone. He had been sleeping very soundly; he had taken a powerful sleeping pill to overcome his insomnia. The pill had not yet worn off and he still felt groggy. Half awake, he picked up the receiver and said, "Hello—who's there?"

"This is the reception desk. Comrade Yi Yang is here to see you."

Rong was immediately alert. Yi Yang had been successful and famous for many years. Even now, his newest works were widely displayed and appreciated, and his name often appeared in the reviews and articles of art critics. He was like the largest gem in an emperor's crown, eternally and brilliantly gleaming. His paintings were known for their excellence of composition, his brushwork considered exquisite. But . . . his paintings always left people feeling that there was something human missing from them. They were perfect but emotionless. There was always a distance between the painter and his painting. In spite of this, people could easily see how much energy Yi Yang put into his work. It presented a strange conundrum: While he seemed never to put all his heart into his work, he obviously took it very seriously and perfected his technique. At Mrs. Hassen's banquet the day before, the two artists had nodded and shaken hands, but they had had no chance to talk. Today, Yi Yang with his titles and reputation had come to the hotel to see him; it made Rong rather nervous.

"Please ask him to come right up."

Rong hung up the phone and jumped out of bed. He stuck his head under the cold water and washed hastily. That awakened him thoroughly. He dressed quickly. Just as he drew on his long underwear, there was a knock at the door. It would not be polite to leave such an important man standing in the hall, so Rong rushed to the door and opened it. How could he have known that there would be at least ten men and women accompanying Yi Yang? Before he could take the situation in, the group came forward and into his room—there was no time for him to close the door.

Rong was humiliated. He held his coat in front of him. These people were so absorbed in their efforts to make themselves known to Rong, they seemed to take no notice of the fact that he was not fully clothed. They acted as if he might at any moment become a puff of smoke and disappear. A woman wearing a red wool sweater began before anyone else had a chance and introduced the man who knew everything. "This is the head of the Cultural Center. . . ."

The woman in the silk jacket did not wish to appear inferior and did her best to compete, introducing her own leader, "This is the editor in chief of the art and literature supplement of X paper."

The head of the Cultural Center said, "This is a new star in the literary sphere—have you read her novel *Heart*,

Don't Beat So Hard? And this is a singing star—she's just finished recording a new album. . . ."

The newspaper editor interrupted and played his ace. "This is a theater star; she's just appeared as the lead in *Mandarin Ducks in a Dream*. And here's the newest rising star in the world of fine arts. Her painting *Lonely Moon* has been sent to Beijing. . . ."

Good heavens. It seemed these leaders had a special interest in running a school for young women only— where were the men in G City? How fortunate this city would be if all these beautiful young women were to inherit their ancestors' reputations and glory in all these fields. Surely, a propitious star was shining over it.

Rong found himself surrounded by bright smiles from these hearts, moons and Mandarin ducks; he felt like a cornered beast. Each smile was bright, and taken together they were so dazzling he could hardly keep his eyes open.

It was Yi Yang who helped him out of this predicament. "Let's allow Comrade Rong Chang Lan to finish dressing." All at once everyone noticed the bright red long underwear and the bare feet with their thick, raw joints. Rong shot Yi Yang a look of gratitude and escaped into the bathroom. Behind him exploded a symphony of laughter—high and low, smooth and rough, thick and thin.

The women, each in her own way, loudly tried to comfort the frightened rabbit.

"Oh, as an artist you needn't be so conservative!"

"Don't worry, you lose nothing by our having seen this!"

"You're wearing more here than you would in a swimming pool."

Oh, these terrible new females! These women would undoubtedly love working as masseuses in a foreign massage parlor. Rong stepped into his trousers and sat on the edge of the tub and worried about going back out. He would have preferred to hide somewhere. But Yi Yang was out there waiting for him; Rong would have to force himself to leave the sanctuary of the bathroom for his sake. He felt safe only when he was standing beside Yi Yang.

"At the banquet yesterday I didn't have a chance to tell you how much pleasure your paintings gave me. I felt compelled to come here and tell you how I felt, like an enthusiastic young person." Then he introduced his companion to Rong. "Comrade Huang Zui." The introduction was short and rather formal, lacking any list of credits. This seemed to set her apart, above all the "stars." There was nothing eager about the gesture when she offered her hand to shake Rong's.

" 'Zui' may mean 'overdrink,' but I don't drink at all," she explained.

"I would like to take you to meet all the older generation of artists and the leaders in every field who will be useful to you. You may not realize this, but people here in G City are not very well informed and they respond slowly to new things. I hope people will understand your work quickly." Yi Yang's words were well chosen and well expressed.

Every sentence he spoke drew the attention of these hearts, moons and Mandarin ducks, and won him their boundless admiration. Yi Yang was the only genuine star in the room.

Huang Zui took this opportunity to say, "I would like

to invite you to come to my home whenever you are free. Father likes to become acquainted with people in fine-arts and literary circles. He does calligraphy when he has time. Here's our telephone number; please call me when you know when you can come. I'll send the car to pick you up. I have no brothers or sisters, and being alone I feel lonely. . . ."

The young literary star found her tongue and hastily approached Rong, saying, "Comrade Rong, we would like you to give us a lecture at the Cultural Center when you have time."

The young painter said, "I would be very grateful if you would let me be your student. Tomorrow I will bring my portfolio for you to look over."

Huang Zui laughed and said, "You have asked every famous painter in the province to teach you, haven't you? Aren't you worried that your painting will be a combination of too many styles—a hybrid?"

The young painter had a quick tongue and showed herself quite capable of a skillful riposte. "Why do you say that? I can't compete with you. Painting, music, fine arts—you've tried your hand at all these; you have quite a collection of 'brothers.' "

Huang Zui replied, "Are you jealous? If you are, you'll just have to try harder."

The singer and the actress looked unhappy; they saw no opportunity to enter the conversation.

While Huang Zui and the painter were busy with each other, the girl in the silk jacket seized the opportunity to give Rong her name and address and to express succinctly her interest and admiration.

The room had become a battlefield, with women doing the fighting.

Yi Yang was silent. He was not watching the women, he was watching Rong Chang Lan. Clearly Rong was no match for these women. The subtle smile that played at the corners of Yi Yang's mouth went undetected by everyone in the room.

Wu Zhi Heng arrived at precisely eleven-thirty. "Aha, here are the hero and the heroines together!" He nodded, shook hands and bowed to everyone; no one questioned the artful compliments he paid—they were just pleased to receive them. He didn't neglect the singer and the actress, who had been rather left out, nor the two cultural leaders who had been forgotten since their introduction. At exactly twelve, Wu stood up and said, "Now it's time for lunch, but none of you need give that a thought. We'll all eat together in the dining room."

"Oh . . . how nice . . . very good . . ." The women jumped and chirped as cheerfully as birds. Then the squadron set off for the hotel dining room. Like a rolling snowball, the group grew larger as it went through the halls, gathering to itself acquaintances met along the way. The hotel seemed to be the culture club of the province.

Everyone wanted to sit at one large table, to share the distinction of sitting with Yi Yang and Rong Chang Lan. The waiters had to push together five square tables to form one large one. The women skirmished secretly for the privilege of sitting on either side of Rong.

"Today we have ladies with us, so the meal should be especially fine," said Wu.

"Of course . . ." Rong agreed. He was thinking it was a

good thing he had that two thousand yuan to rely on. He was told that Mrs. Hassen was ready to buy another of his paintings. He could only hope that was true.

People kept standing up and offering toasts. Reasonable toasts at first, but as the afternoon wore on they became more and more extravagant. As the number of empty bottles increased, the toasts lost more and more of their polish. The party was drawing the attention of the other diners as the toasts grew louder and more reckless, all of the revelers trying to make sure the onlookers would know who they were and whom they were toasting.

Rong slid lower and lower into his chair. He would gladly have slid all the way under the table. The woman in the silk jacket whispered to him in a concerned voice, "If you're feeling uncomfortable, I'd be happy to accompany you upstairs."

This offer scared him sufficiently to make him immediately straighten his back against the chair. "No, thanks. . . . It doesn't matter. . . . I'm fine."

The meal seemed hopelessly interminable to Rong. He thought they would keep eating till the end of the world. The meal might never have ended if the head of the Cultural Center had not become drunk and said something insulting to the chief editor, which nearly resulted in a fight.

The people finally dispersed, and Rong escaped like a defeated general retreating in such haste that he had no time to consider what route to take. His head was splitting and felt ready to burst, but he found the energy to get up to his room, where he collapsed on his sofa.

"Are you tired? If not, I'd like to stay and talk for a

while." Wu checked his watch. "It's three-thirty now, and at four the hot water will be turned on. I want to stay and take a bath."

Rong was very tired. He had wanted to sleep for a while, but how could he refuse to let a guest stay?

"Right. Sit down. I'm not tired." Looking at Wu's sweaty, oily face, which had gotten that way from drinking and eating and toasting and shouting, Rong realized Wu really did need a bath.

"I never talk to people or make a nuisance of myself without good reason." Wu slumped on the sofa and leaned his head back. He stretched his long legs and rested his feet on the tea table, apparently settling in for a long conversation. "What's your impression of Yi Yang?"

"I think he really wants to look after me."

"There's an old story that's too old to be any older. People have been telling this story for thousands of years, but they go on repeating it again and again."

"What story?"

"The story about the fox and the sour grapes."

"You mean Yi Yang—but you're good friends, aren't you?"

"I mean nothing. I would say that the relations between these people and me are neither good nor bad. Do you read the newspapers?"

"Of course I do."

"Haven't you learned anything from recent history? Look at those men who just accomplished that coup d'état—they were all highly trusted subordinates of the man they overthrew."

"You mean Yi Yang . . ."

"I mean nothing. They are trying to wear Mrs. Hassen

down. Do you know how many people are eyeing this opportunity to go abroad? Don't think you've won so easily. There are many people who are very good at using the soft touch and then the hard. . . . They don't give up until they get what they're after. They go on working until they make a foreigner lose patience and let them have their own way. The foreigner finally gives in rather than suffer a nervous breakdown."

"If there's an opportunity to go abroad and study to enrich my knowledge and experience and to open my eyes to broader horizons, of course that would be very good. But if I can't go, there's nothing to be annoyed about."

"You sound like a good socialist; your motives are very high and altruistic. Some people speak continually of 'the dignity of the country' and 'discipline,' but in their bones they are the slaves of foreigners. I'll give you a simple example: When a delegation is being sent abroad, there are some people who would beg, borrow or steal to get to go too. Don't believe for a moment the high-sounding words they speak or their criticisms of other people's motives or morality. Who knows whether their words are true or false? If a person is truly innocent, they'll make up a purely fictitious story to bring him down. And once the rumor is spread, nobody bothers to find out whether it's true or not. If someone went so far as to be concerned enough to check on the rumor, it would still be of no use. It would be too late—the damage would already be done. You would have lost your chance. The list of names for the delegation would already have been finalized. No one would wait for you unless you were Picasso. And if it's shown that you are untrustworthy you will not be allowed to go abroad, which just proves that going abroad is used as a special perquisite, a political honor or a reward. Why don't they regard going abroad as a kind of punishment? Because they are the slaves of foreigners. In fact, sometimes the ones who betray the country and desert the delegation are those who were thought most pure and trustworthy by the leaders. Shouldn't this phenomenon receive attention?" Wu Zhi Heng said all this earnestly and vigorously, just as earlier he had earnestly and vigorously drunk and toasted and told jokes with Yi Yang. His face grew more sweaty and oily; his rather thin hair stuck to his forehead in little clumps.

"I'm really not interested in such things."

"You're not interested? But people are interested in you." He stood up. "If you don't believe me, wait and see." Facing Rong, he raised his arm and pointed ahead like a prophet.

There was a light knock at the door. It sounded faintly mysterious, like a wizard's sorcery. They looked at each other, then simultaneously turned toward the door. Rong hesitated, then opened the door. A woman shrank back as he did; a four- or five-year-old boy stood beside her. They both stepped back as if frightened when they saw Rong.

"Who are you looking for?"

"We're . . . ah . . . we're looking for you."

"For me?" Rong was puzzled when he saw her. Her clothes were not especially tidy, her face suggested ill health, and her right hand fumbled with a button on her blouse. He didn't know this woman. "Why are you looking for me?"

"Ah . . . why . . . you don't recognize me? I am Yu Ping." The woman had become angry. She pulled the boy from behind her and pushed him forward to face Rong. "Xiao Ming, say hello to your father."

The boy obviously did not want to say anything, but the woman kept poking her finger into his back, forcing him to speak. Reluctantly, he said, "Father," then hid himself again.

Rong Chang Lan almost fainted. He tried to correct the mistake. "You've confused me with someone else."

Wu came up to them and asked, "What's the matter?"

The woman's expression changed. She became fierce and tough, and shouted, "You think I've made a mistake and think you're someone else? I would know you even if you were reduced to ash!" The other guests on the ninth floor could hear her shouting and were curious. One after another, doors opened and heads craned to see what was going on.

Acting quickly, Wu pulled the woman and her child into the room. "Come in, please. Now calm down, and speak slowly."

Wu settled the woman on the sofa. She stretched her mouth grotesquely and began to cry. "It was so difficult to find you," she sobbed. "You're so coldhearted. You went away and never returned. I thought I'd never see you again, and I wouldn't have if I hadn't recognized your picture in the newspaper."

"This . . . what . . . what does this mean?" Rong was very worried. He stood there rubbing his hands together and shuffling his feet. There was a ringing in his ears and a floating feeling had come over him. He looked pleadingly at Wu, who returned a look that said "Calm down." The woman's wailing grew even louder. "You're a really good actor. Look at me again; are you sure you don't recognize me?" She stood up and walked slowly toward Rong. He stepped back. "You took advantage of me when I was young and innocent. When you found out that I was pregnant with this child, you deserted me and I never saw you again. You made me so miserable, and I suffered the condemnation of society. . . . Now you're great and famous and will soon be rich . . . but don't be happy too soon. After you've put me in such a position, you can never be happy. . . ."

The woman spoke so convincingly that Rong wondered if perhaps he had dallied with some innocent girl once upon a time. He began to wonder if the boy might be his own flesh and blood. . . . He even began to see a very strong likeness to himself in the boy. Did this woman have some power by which to turn a fairy tale into reality? Was such a thing really possible? Rong felt the hairs on his body stand on end.

Wu took the woman's arm and led her back to the sofa. "Sit down, and calm down. According to your story, you have a special relationship to Rong Chang Lan. This is a very serious matter, you know. If things are as you say, he will be put on trial. Have you thought about the questions that would be raised by justice? For example: Where and when did you know the defendant? Where and when did this event take place? Are there any witnesses who can attest to your relationship? What exactly was his rank, his occupation, his work unit, his family and his address? . . . We can stop listing questions there, but you will also be asked when his birthday is and which animal sign he was born under. Can you answer these questions correctly? If the ox's head doesn't fit the horse's mouth, you'll be accused of libel, of slander, of calumny. I don't believe you're blackmailing, because there are many people on earth with the same name as Rong Chang Lan." As he spoke he watched the woman's expression. Her crying grew quieter, and she withdrew farther and farther into the corner of the sofa. Wu smiled inwardly; she obviously realized that her ill-conceived story was falling apart. While he secretly laughed at the woman's stupid act, she fell backward and seemed to go into a convulsive fit. Her eyes rolled back and traces of foam appeared at the corners of her mouth. The boy threw himself on her crying, "Mama!"

Rong was so frightened by the situation that he had no idea what to do. "What should we do? What should we do?"

Wu smiled coldly and said, "Don't worry; it's epilepsy. The performance was too stressful for her." He picked up the phone and asked for the hotel doctor. After being given medication, the woman gradually recovered. But she still lay on the sofa with her eyes closed, attempting to get as much sympathy as possible. Wu whispered something into the doctor's ear, and then she was carried out of the room on a stretcher.

The large audience crowded in the hall waited patiently. They had begun to gather when the woman had first knocked at Rong's door, and their patience no doubt would stand the test of infinity.

Mrs. Hassen appeared in time for only the final scene in this drama. Her room key dropped from her hand; frightened, she crossed her arms over her chest as if to protect herself. She looked inquiringly at Rong, but in his eyes she found no recognition. He closed his door without a backward glance. He ran directly into the bathroom, bent over the toilet and retched.

Mrs. Hassen returned to her room, her mind full of suspicion. She sat on her sofa and stared at the opposite wall, confused by events in this strange place.

With regard to technique Rong had obviously sought the style of Western classicism. The otherworldly atmosphere in his painting, his arrangement of light and shadow, the line, and the tones of the colors were sometimes harmonious, sometimes contrastive—all of these things indicated that he would be a master painter. But he preferred to remain an unknown country teacher; he was not interested in seeking glory in the Western world. And his talk about "the soul of a nation," although somewhat naive, earned Mrs. Hassen's respect. Maybe he misunderstood her kindness and believed she was encouraging him to emigrate to the West. An embarrassing thought. In any case, she still respected him.

Mr. Ke, who was in charge of international cultural exchange, looked down on and often criticized Western society and culture. But the people who were negotiating the details of visits abroad asked Mrs. Hassen if, instead of taking Rong Chang Lan alone to her country, she could use the same amount of money, spread thinner, to take two or three people. They suggested that Mr. Ke head the delegation.

"This wasn't our original plan. We only invited a painter. Would Mr. Ke agree to such an arrangement?" Mrs. Hassen deeply believed that Mr. Ke would not wish to visit that rotten, decayed, imperialistic country; it would only make him and everyone else unhappy. "And we would feel sorry to have to lower the standards of Mr. Rong's accommodations—he's such a talented young painter."

"For the sake of our revolutionary work, we need Comrade Ke to make this trip. He will agree."

"Is it necessary to coerce him into going if he doesn't want to?"

"Not coerce. Comrade Ke is of the older generation, of noble character and high prestige; even in national fine-arts circles, he has some degree of influence. He is the only one who can systematically and widely introduce an artist from our province to the West. We hope that you Westerners will gain a broad understanding of us. And as far as the level of Rong's accommodations in your country goes, let's ask him for his opinion. All right?"

"All right." Mrs. Hassen was glad they had made a slight concession on the point of Rong's accommodations. She would wait to hear what he thought. Clearly it would be impossible for her to refuse to invite the additional members of the delegation. She sighed. . . . It was disappointing, though, as if she had invited one special friend to come for dinner and he had arrived bringing several strangers with him. And the money was limited; it would be impossible to increase the sum. What should she do? She was a woman who enjoyed a high position; she lived in ease and comfort. She had never dealt with such a situation before. Her husband had often told her how much easier it was now than it had been to deal with Chinese policies and systems. The people now in charge of every aspect of the government were much easier to cooperate with, were flexible and had courage. Maybe that's how it was in Beijing; here it was different.

———

What should she do? She would have to make a long-distance call to Beijing—perhaps her husband could help.

A person loves a painter's work and wants to share it with other people. It had seemed such a simple thing at first. But now she felt as if she had fallen into quicksand, and it was becoming impossible to get out.

5

He had become plumper—noticeably plumper. His eyes seemed smaller and the tip of his nose sank even deeper behind his thick protruding lips. Could it be that he had already grown plumper from eating and drinking every day and never doing anything?

It was a shame. He had applied to return to his small village. He still had students to teach and paintings to paint. He had in mind a very good idea for a painting. He had told Yi Yang that if he got his idea onto canvas, he was sure it would be good enough to be put on display in Beijing.

But the authorities responsible did not agree. "You want to leave G City while Mrs. Hassen is still here? The arrangements have not been finalized yet. How can you leave?"

Rong did not see what connection he had with all of that. He had finished all he had wanted to do in G City, so why couldn't he leave? It was like being under house arrest. The authorities had telephoned his village and mailed an official letter asking that Rong be given an extended leave so that he could stay in G City longer. The County Bureau of Culture and Education had agreed directly. "For the sake of the revolutionary work, Rong

Chang Lan may stay as long as you need him." What did it matter if the students missed some of their fine-arts lessons?

"You want to paint? Just paint here."

Yi Yang brought his own easels, brushes and pigments to the hotel.

Rong was grateful to Yi Yang for his care and thoughtfulness, but how could he paint in such a place?

He was also disturbed by another pressing matter. There seemed to be a great power pressuring him to get married.

The women had begun coming to his room earlier and earlier every day, and leaving later and later. Each one seemed afraid that if she left him unaccompanied another woman would take advantage of the opening. He had to get up earlier and go to bed later to avoid being caught in his quilt. His eyelids were puffy from lack of sleep. But it was difficult to ask his guests to leave; even when he did they would act as if they had not heard him. Strange, but the attendants were not so careful about bringing in boiled water and cleaning the room at odd hours anymore. Now Rong was always wishing for the attendants' appearance. But maybe they guarded against contact between the sexes only when one of the parties was foreign. They seemed to give the green light to Chinese women.

The women followed him wherever he went. They were like an impenetrable wall that even water could not have flowed through. They made it impossible for him to contact or talk with his classmates and teachers in the college of fine arts. His whole life was lived completely in public; the only privacy he had was in going to the john.

On the one hand, he hated them deeply, felt trapped by

them and sometimes actually wanted to beat them out of his door with his fists. But on the other, he was a man, and sometimes his heart beat faster and he could not help being attracted by these women.

He didn't know which of them would be the best choice. Each of them had made him feel that only she could be his future wife—that only she could combine her hair with his.

They were fighting to win the throne of Mrs. Rong, or rather the position of Mrs. Rong, who would accompany her husband abroad. They fought most viciously when in his presence. They exposed each other's secrets unmercifully and without forgiveness; they all seemed to have an equal share of secrets. It seemed that by abusing another woman, a woman took upon herself a greater degree of purity. They were all grasping at him so tightly that he felt they would tear him into many pieces.

Peach-colored rumors about the eligible bachelor Rong spread throughout G City. Comrade Ke sighed and said worriedly to Yi Yang, "Is it true?"

"It's just some bored busybody who doesn't have anything better to do than to spread this silly tale all through town. Why must people interfere in another person's private life? On this point I agree with the Western idea that the individual has a right to privacy; his personal life is no one's business but his own."

"Just let him go home," Comrade Ke said in exasperation.

"How can we do that? If we let him go home, will Mrs. Hassen still be interested in our negotiations?" Yi Yang's words, like his paintings, were carefully arranged.

"But if he continues in this way in G City we can't trust

him to behave properly while he's abroad. The circumstances would be infinitely more complicated abroad, and someone with so little self-control could make some terrible mistakes."

"Aren't we trying to send two or three additional people along with Rong?"

"Yes, we are. Many comrades have advised me to head the delegation—they are looking at this from the political angle. The truth is, I don't have any interest whatsoever in going abroad. But I am an 'older comrade,' and I must consider what's best for the Party and put aside my own wishes."

"What you say is exactly right. But your health . . . traveling abroad can be very taxing, so we should be sure that there's a younger, stronger person with you to help you. Someone who is capable and upon whom you could depend whenever you needed him."

Yi Yang's words could not have been any clearer or more tactfully chosen to reveal his abilities. Ke said, "It would save me a lot of energy and worry if you could go."

"Oh, no, no. It's very kind of you to suggest it, but I'm really not worthy of such a compliment. It makes me feel a bit nervous and uneasy for you to say such things."

"And . . . if he did marry right now that would create a lot of complications for us, a lot of complications. So I think he'd better leave here as soon as possible."

"But what use is there in letting him go home? We should first finalize plans with Mrs. Hassen and make sure of the names for the delegation. . . ."

Just then the telephone rang. The man in charge of the negotiations told Ke that Mrs. Hassen had agreed to

invite three people abroad, since Rong had insisted he
would prefer to have them along and was quite willing to
give up some luxury. She would fly to Beijing tomorrow.
"Please arrange today's farewell banquet—and make it
sumptuous." Comrade Ke hung up the receiver and said
with satisfaction, "Mm—good."

"If I've got my bearings straight, the trip has been
arranged for the latter half of the year. Rong could then
spend the remaining months producing more paintings of
a high enough quality to take abroad. He has discussed
some of his concepts for future paintings with me—he
really is a talented man. We should treasure his talent.
He's still young and doesn't know how to protect himself;
he could easily be destroyed by either excess praise or
criticism. Perhaps it would be good to just let him return
to that small village where life is more simple and pure."
Yi Yang had learned that Huang Zui had been compara-
tively successful with Rong. And her father seemed to
approve of the marriage. If it were actually accomplished,
then there would be even more flowers on Rong Chang
Lan's brocade. Yi Yang was deeply disturbed by the
thought.

"Mm—good. Let him go home right away." Ke felt
that Yi Yang's every action demonstrated his experience,
talent and ability. He had worked with Yi Yang for many
years and had found that whatever the trouble or difficulty, Yi Yang was always able to resolve the situation and
free him. He was a gem. More and more Ke felt that he
must never lose Yi Yang.

But before Mrs. Hassen left, the entire situation
changed dramatically.

At the banquet Yi Yang personally invited Rong to

drink with him three times, toasting him as a close friend. Rong would have declined to drink with anyone else, but he couldn't refuse Yi Yang. After all, for a close friend, one would even sacrifice one's life. They were drinking *maotai*, very strong wine, and the glasses were not small. After three glasses of *maotai* Rong was soused. He could never remember afterward whether he had drunk anything more than the three *maotais*. In any case, he was drunk—roaring drunk. He imitated a rooster crowing and a dog howling; he used his fingers like chopsticks to stir food around and pick it up. Mrs. Hassen was sitting beside him, her face changing from white to red and back again. People exchanged angry and accusing looks.

Yi Yang and another man took Rong upstairs to his room, helped him take off his shoes and tucked him under his quilt. They put a cup of hot tea on his bedside table. "Have a good rest." They patted him affectionately on the shoulder and left. "He's so innocent and lovable," Yi Yang said to Mrs. Hassen.

"He once told me that he didn't drink," said Mrs. Hassen.

"Ah . . . is that so? I never knew him to lie before. I'm sure he only behaved that way because he had too much to drink. Please forgive him."

At that moment, Rong's room was in upheaval. He was only dimly aware that someone came to his bedside—like a cloud of incense. The scent made him even drowsier. The cloud surrounded him and turned to dew that fell on his cheek and lips and burned where it fell. He felt so comfortable. The stinking mixture in his stomach seemed to make him more eager to inhale this incense.

But suddenly it all disappeared. He could make out

only the shadowy outlines of two people dodging around his room—they were fighting, yelling indistinguishable oaths. Rong tried to get up to find out exactly what was happening. He thought the two wrestling figures were Huang Zui and the young woman writer. Why were they fighting, and why were they in his room? How strange. He wanted to stand up and separate them, but his feet became tangled in the carpet and he fell. He slept soundly where he landed. It was impossible to awaken him. Even after the woman writer had smashed a lamp over Huang Zui's head and the room filled with people, Rong slept.

After this came the local police station, detention, trial and prosecution. Rong would never know that all of these steps had been orchestrated by Yi Yang to help Huang Zui. It had not been Yi Yang's idea; Huang Zui had cried and pleaded for "Uncle Yi" to help her get revenge on the woman writer. The defendant was the writer, obviously not Rong Chang Lan, because Yi Yang was Rong's friend, and even more because Huang Zui was infatuated with him.

Very soon afterward it was announced that Rong Chang Lan's authorization to go abroad had been revoked. At the same time, his room became quiet. All the women disappeared without a trace. And the writer Wu Zhi Heng didn't come either. Only Yi Yang came—often. "Don't be so upset, you are still young, and you have a long life full of opportunities ahead of you," Yi Yang comforted and advised him. But he didn't tell Rong that the list of delegation members had been decided and that it consisted of Ke Yi Yun and his son and Yi Yang himself.

Now Rong could relax—he slept soundly for three

whole days. On the morning of the fourth day he received a telegram from the County Bureau of Culture and Education ordering him to return immediately and await punishment.

He bought his train ticket and checked out of the hotel. After paying his bill, he had exactly seven yuan eighty left out of the two thousand yuan. He was quite satisfied; this sum was enough to cover his trip home. He took off his gray polyester Western suit like an actor taking off his costume and put it into his green canvas bag. Then he put on his old small jacket. He felt relieved, and walked out of the room that seemed like a magic box.

No one came to see him off. It was as if no one knew he was leaving. When he entered the elevator, he heard a familiar male voice behind him. "This is the most satisfactory cleaning job I've ever had done."

A woman's voice asked, "You had it cleaned 'over there,' didn't you?"

"Yes, I did. It cost twenty marks, which is equivalent to more than ten yuan."

Rong turned his head—it was the man with the "fool's camera." Apparently he had just returned from Germany. He still wore thick hair grease and that dark Western suit. The suit that had cost twenty marks to clean didn't look any better than before to Rong. It still wasn't long enough where it ought to be long and wasn't short enough where it ought to be short; it wasn't fitted enough where it ought to be fitted and wasn't loose enough where it ought to be loose. But the man's spirits and self-confidence were very different from what they had been when he was showing his camera to the desk clerk. From the elevator Rong walked directly toward the hotel gate.

He walked away feeling like a free man. He could never have been mistaken for a hotel porter and asked to carry luggage.

"Comrade Rong Chang Lan!" He heard someone call his name. He turned and saw Wu Zhi Heng. He had stood up from where he had been sitting on the long bench by the reception desk and was walking toward him slowly. "I've come especially to see you off."

They walked out of the hotel together and took the bus to the train station. On the bus, in the waiting room and on the platform they were silent. It was uncomfortable just to stand face to face without speaking, so together they paced the length of the platform.

As the train pulled into the station, Wu finally spoke. "Do you feel sad?"

"No. Of course not. This has been an enriching experience."

"That's right, I think it's been very good for you, and you will paint better in the future. The otherworldly feeling—plus realism."

The train drew slowly up to the platform. The men shook hands in silence. Wu Zhi Heng handed a brown envelope to Rong. He did not wait to see the train leave.

Rong Chang Lan opened the envelope. Inside he found two hundred yuan and this simple sentence: "I think this may be useful to you." Rong smiled and put the money back into the envelope. He recalled a phrase people in the countryside were fond of repeating at New Year's when they would superstitiously smash a bowl or two: "Break a possession and keep catastrophe away." As the train sped toward the fields, Rong's spirits began to improve.

But his whole body began to itch, and he scratched his

waist and back and under his arms—yet it did no good. The itching persisted all over his body and would not be stopped. He could not get comfortable either sitting or standing. He felt very uneasy. He went into the toilet, took off his small jacket and examined it closely. In the seams and throughout the fibers of the cloth he found countless lice and their eggs.

Translated by Deborah J. Leonard
and Zhang Andong

⤚ Something Else?

I NEVER want to see him again. He's a bastard.
He kicked me so hard yesterday that my ribs are still hurting.

And I didn't even do anything wrong—I didn't steal any food from the kitchen. I must admit that from time to time I do take a little something, but how's a cat meant to survive otherwise? I didn't tear or chew that tattered string bag hanging from the doorknob, the way I used to. Admittedly I'm always on the lookout for something to amuse me, but it's not much fun playing with that old bag. Any day now I'll be completely fed up with it.

Several days ago I dropped into a neighbor's. I saw the calico cat there playing with a small white ball. When the ball rolled, it made the most intriguing sound. It was almost impossible for us to pick it up or hold it in our mouths. The ball just kept rolling and spinning in front of us, tempting us to pick it up. What fun it was! I would so love to have a ball like that to play with. But I'm sure if he knew, he'd say, "Hmpf! Now you want a ball—you should be happy with what you have!"

He likes nothing better than to scold me and tell me that I should be content with what I have.

WHENEVER he's in a bad mood he takes it out on me. It's so unfair—when I'm in a bad mood, who can I take it out on? He thinks that since I'm only an animal he can be as cruel to me as he wants because I can't really fight back. And if he went as far as to kick me to death, so what? No one would hold a funeral for a cat. I would be very easy to replace—there are a lot of cats in the world. My mother had four of us in one litter alone, and none of us could escape the fate of depending on humans for food. When I think of this, I wish all the cats in the world would die at once—then what would men find to play with? When his face grows as dark as a pickled eel's tail and he slouches on the sofa, his long legs stretched out wide apart, and he leans his big head back and stares at the ceiling, you can bet he's either in a bad mood or devising some plot. When he's like that it's best to stay well out of his way. Yesterday I failed to get away when he was in such a mood and so I got kicked.

He gets in these moods two or three times a week. When this one began, it was terrible—all hell suddenly broke loose. And then, before I could even figure out what was happening, his mood abruptly changed and he was all smiles. It's almost like when we cats fight—there's a lot of spitting and hissing and then suddenly it's all over. Once or twice I have known the causes of his outbursts, and they were quite trivial—things as insubstantial as chicken feathers and garlic skins. Being nervous and hypersensitive, he drives himself into terrible furies—he makes his own gods and devils.

———

"Kitty!" He calls me and taps my dish. The scent of fish rises quickly to my nostrils, and my mouth begins to water. I clench my teeth and hold my breath and refuse to respond.

"Kitty!" Still calling. After he sees that I don't respond, he begins poking me in the belly and tickling me under my shoulders. "Hey—look—we've spoiled this cat. Fish isn't good enough for him anymore!"

Nonsense! Who's he trying to fool? When did he ever give me the fish's body? It's always only heads and tails for me.

Don't get me wrong; I'm not asking for more. . . . If he gives me fish heads and tails to eat, that's as it should be. He's my master; of course he should eat the main part of the fish. It wouldn't be right if he gave himself the heads and tails, and me the body. If that ever happened I'm sure I'd think he'd lost his mind. What I can't bear is the way he gives them to me, the way he tells me to eat them. When he speaks, it's as if he's implying that if he did give me the best part of the fish to eat, I'd still not be satisfied and would pick through it, eating only the most desirable morsels. As if I wouldn't even know when I had it good. Am I the sort of creature who's so self-centered that he doesn't know how high the sky is or how deep the earth is? I never expect more than my due. I'm a cat who knows his place.

I open one eye a crack and regard him coldly. His face is shiny, like the belly of a fish, and it's obvious that he's in a good mood today. I can read him like a book. No matter how well-bred and gentlemanly he may try to appear in front of others, I know how uncouth he really is. For instance, I have even seen him eating fried pastry while he's going to the toilet. He doesn't need to put on a good face for me, because I'm only a cat. Who ever heard of a man being concerned about behaving well for his animal? I'm convinced most men would behave very differently from their public images when hidden away from all eyes, including those of their wives and children. That's why so many like to go home and remain in the privacy of a darkened room. It frees them from all inhibitions.

When he feels bored or depressed he tortures me for entertainment. Sometimes he holds his cigarette close to my face, sending the smoke into my eyes. Sometimes he rubs menthol oil on my nose. Sometimes he spits into my mouth or puts chili on my tongue. There are times when he picks me up by my head and dangles me in the air, twisting my head around like a screw. I've been truly scared that my neck would snap and my head would come right off in his hand. Once I cried out in pain and used my front paws to claw and my back legs to kick. I tried my best to free myself. He struck my paws and, when he saw that I was quite helpless, laughed himself silly.

It's true that on occasion he does actually play with me for a few minutes at a time. He wiggles his fingers for me to try to catch them. I wait for just the right moment and then spring up to catch them. He instantly raises his hand out of reach and I leap with as much power as I have, higher than I ever imagined I could. At such moments I'm proud of my strength. In reality, his fingers are not my goal. Even if I did reach them I would give them only a gentle bite and then run away to prepare for the next leap. In those leaps I can feel my agility, my strength and my limitless vitality. In those moments I feel I'm a real cat, and not just a worthless wretch to be kneaded and shaped by him, dependent on him for food and shelter. Then I can forgive him for all his cruelty to me. I don't like to bear grudges. I'm a kind cat—I daresay he could never find one kinder.

But in the midst of our play, he'll suddenly dodge aside so that I plunge into the darkness of the bathroom, and he slams the door shut behind me. No matter how hard I cry and beg to be let out, he never responds.

I cry and shout because I feel frightened. I'm not afraid of the dark—to a cat's eyes there's no real difference between night and day. We don't make the clear distinctions between night and day that humans make.

The bathroom is narrow and small, and it seems to me that the ceiling is very high. Except for the toilet, the room is empty. When there's nothing to look at, we fall back on our imagination. That's why I'm frightened. I don't know where my thoughts will lead. And so I risk my life to cry out for release. At least I'm doing something that will keep my thoughts away from my fearful imaginings. When I'm in this situation—either because of the walls or something more ominous—my voice never sounds like my own. Feelings that it would take a psychologist to explain seem magnified and reflected back to me at ten times their normal size. *Aiya!* And that only makes me all the more frightened. The more frightened I become, the harder I cry and the more frightened I become. Sometimes I'm so scared, my fur stands on end. I wish someone would open that door—I would be eternally grateful and kowtow to him!

HE stands up and walks away from me, singing a tune from Peking Opera: "Last night . . . I had a dream . . ."

and goes on to hum the tune played on the *huqin*. Always humming the accompaniment—when will he get on with the next sentence of the opera? Hmm—I know that in fact he can sing only this one line. How many years has he been singing it? Probably my mother's and my grandmother's generations have had to suffer it. And maybe my sons and grandsons will also have to listen to it. Perhaps I expect too much. Of course, I do things wrong sometimes and I am discontented with my lot. It's not so terrible that he can sing only one sentence. After all, he's not a Peking Opera singer. I can't even sing a single word. It's not important; his wife still seems to love him, and his son still takes his orders. It doesn't really concern me, does it?

After walking around the room, he comes and pinches my nose. I use my paw to push away his hand gently as I give a big sneeze. But he continues to pinch me. I stand up—can I get away? He grabs me by the tail and fiercely drags me backward. It hurts so much that I turn around and bite his hand. Not a hard bite. He hits me very hard and I run under the bed and hide in a space between two boxes. I'm sure he won't be able to reach me here. So I stay in my little hiding place and wait.

I don't know how much time has passed, because I fell asleep. It's dark outside now and the lamps are lit. I'm very hungry and will have to slip out from under the bed and eat my fish head and tail. While I eat, I laugh scornfully at myself. If I think my master is so bad, I should leave him. But if I leave, how do I know whether I will ever have even fish heads and tails to eat? What's more, I worry that the Cantonese family upstairs will catch me, strip my fur and eat my meat. The calico cat warned me once: "Beware of that Cantonese family up-stairs: they eat anything, mice, snakes, monkeys—and I've even heard they eat cats!"

Well. I suppose I had better stay here and try to be satisfied. The grass isn't always greener on the other side. . . . And even after all I've said, he could be worse.

Translated by Deborah J. Leonard
and Zhang Andong

✄ Today's Agenda

✄ *One Morning in July,*
Two Hours Before the Regular Bureau Meeting

"COMRADE Jia, how do you do? How are you feel-ing these days?" Lao Wang welcomed him re-spectfully at the gatehouse.

Comrade Jia, the bureau head, had been away from his office, resting at home for more than a month, trying to lower his high blood pressure.

"Not very well at all," Jia Yunshan replied testily.

AS soon as he had awakened that morning, his wife had told him there was no water and she didn't know when it would come back on. And the office that managed the houses in their large courtyard compound had no infor-mation either. There wasn't a single drop of water in any faucet in the house. They couldn't prepare breakfast, and worse, they couldn't even wash or brush their teeth till the young maid returned. She had gone to the vegetable market on the corner to fill a bucket at the faucet outside the market.

"What can I get you for breakfast?" his wife asked worriedly.

Jia Yunshan's preferences in food were simple and

unvarying. For breakfast there had to be two bowls of millet gruel and one plate of pickled cucumber. Even though the food industry had developed and a wide choice of food was now available, he never deviated from his millet gruel and cucumber. On this point he was immovable; thunder and lightning would be insufficient to shake him from his accustomed breakfast. This is called habit. Habits are very difficult to break. Change often leads to a feeling of uneasiness, uneasiness soon leads to unhappiness. When people are unhappy, their troubles seem to multiply. For example, Bureau Chief Jia's wife was very worried about her husband's blood pressure going up again. Jia Yunshan didn't answer her question. He picked up the telephone receiver and said to the operator, "Put me through to the Department of Housing Management."

The telephone rang for a long time. Again and again Jia Yunshan raised his left arm, looking impatiently at his wristwatch. He let the phone ring for thirteen minutes and still no one answered. Jia Yunshan's face had been blue and white; now it was red.

The operator came on the line: "There's no answer at the Department of Housing Management."

"Keep trying—get me through to someone there." According to the rules, this office was required to have someone on duty at all times. There was no one else to contact if the courtyard was suddenly without water or electricity.

At six forty-five someone at last answered. "Who do you want?" a sleepy-voiced man asked.

"This is Jia Yunshan."

"Who?"

"Jia-Yun-Shan."

At the other end of the line there was a long silence. Maybe he was searching his memory for a face to attach to these three words. Finally, a lazy voice said, "I don't recognize that name. What do you want?"

The name became meaningless in the face of such ignorance. The secretary of the City Party Committee is very important, isn't he? Let him try to take a crowded bus, and he will be pushed and shoved along with everyone else. If the conductor thinks him an eyesore, or not quick enough about climbing into the bus, she might deliberately open and close the doors on him several times, making sure they squeeze him. And just let him try to go shopping—if he has to disturb the chatting shop assistants they will pour out a stream of abuse like dog's blood over his head, as if he were just any customer. Even if he hangs a sign from his neck with his name emblazoned on it, it won't make any difference. Many citizens of this city never read a book or a newspaper, and they wouldn't know whether this man sold onions or garlic.

"I want to know why you didn't inform us that the water would be turned off this morning."

"We did notify . . ." the man was evidently too lazy to bother finishing his sentence.

"Where did you put the notice?"

"Main gate."

"I didn't see it."

"Either the glue was too weak, or the wind was too strong. It blew away." The words were immediately followed by the click of the receiver being hung up. Obviously the man was eager to return to his dreams.

The young maid had returned. Jia Yunshan washed his face and brushed his teeth. With only one basinful of water, he felt compelled to wash as sparingly as possible. When he had finished, his hands and face still felt dirty.

The maid stood waiting for his instructions about breakfast. Jia thought for a few minutes, then said, "Go and buy some soybean milk and some *youtiao*."★

The small shop specializing in soybean milk and *youtiao* was nearby, and although Jia and his wife waited for a very long time, the maid didn't return. Jia looked at his watch; his wife became more worried. "I'll go look for her and see what's taking her so long."

At seven forty-five Jia's wife returned, hand to her chest, breathing heavily. "The line is very long. There were at least thirty people ahead of us, not counting those who cut in. The line behind us stretched for at least one *li*."†

"Why were you so foolishly stubborn—you could have gone to another shop!"

"Another shop? Are there any other shops nearby? I would have to go at least five blocks to find another, and who's to say the line there wouldn't be at least two *li* long!"

"All right, then. I won't eat."

With the most basic requirements for the welfare of the people still not met, Jia Yunshan went to his office to

---

★ *Translators' note:* Fried pastry.

† *Translators' note:* About a third of a mile.

---

attend his meeting. You can imagine what frame of mind he was in when he left home.

WHEN Jia answered, "Not very well at all," Lao Wang looked more carefully at him. His face looked dark and gloomy. Lao Wang said with sympathy, "You should take care to rest, the weather is so hot. Why did you choose today of all days to come back to work?"

Ah, thought Jia, Lao Wang couldn't know that we have an urgent item on today's agenda—the policies for improved treatment of intellectuals. It seemed to Jia that ever since he'd assumed this position, he was always dealing with "urgent matters."

After hearing Lao Wang's caring words, Jia felt he'd spoken too roughly to him. He thought how little effort it would cost him to go into the gatehouse and show a friendly interest in Lao Wang.

Things had changed a lot in the month he'd been gone. The old sofa was gone and a new, sectional sofa was in its place. Each section was on casters so it could be moved easily. The imitation-wool cover was a brown-and-tan plaid. The walls had been painted milk white, and the window and door curtains were coordinated to blend with the walls.

A pleasant scent filled the room. Jia sniffed the air. "What's that sweet smell?"

"Ha—perfume. The Plant Services Department sprays the room with perfume regularly. As you can see, we are keeping in step with the Four Modernizations. You must take a look at the negotiating room." Lao Wang led Jia out of the gatehouse. The air inside the office building was

very cool. When Lao Wang opened the door to the negotiating room, the air that flowed out was even cooler
and fresher. "Ha—air-conditioning. Look at the carpet
and the antimacassars. . . . Do you think they're good
enough? If a foreigner came here to negotiate, I'm sure
he'd think it was almost exactly like home."

Jia nodded and asked, "Is the room used a lot?"

"Ha—it hasn't been opened yet."

Jia began to look more closely at Lao Wang. Why
did he chuckle that way all the time? Those chuckles
seemed rich with implication. The look on Lao Wang's
face seemed foolish rather than honest and open, ignorant
rather than innocent.

"Just go on with your work, I'll go along upstairs." Jia
tactfully said good-bye to his guide and began to climb
the steps. The higher he climbed, the farther behind he
left the cool air. The hot air in front of him seemed to be
forcing the cool air away. Maybe this is how a popsicle
feels when it melts, thought Jia.

When he reached the second floor he felt it was where
he belonged.

The walls were dark gray. You could only glimpse the
original color where the wall had been scraped by some
sharp object.

The hall smelled of mildew. Everything here was
damp; it had rained every day lately. Jia took out his key
and opened his office door. Dust was everywhere. In a
corner were several cobwebs; in the middle of one sat a
spider. The web looked exquisitely delicate in the morning sunshine. How free and happy that spider must be.
He can build a home wherever he wants.

At eight-ten, twenty minutes before the meeting, Jia

realized that because of the string of unexpected problems that morning he had not had time to go to the toilet; he decided to take a few minutes now to relieve this problem. There was a sharp smell of onion in the washroom. There was currently a vegetable shortage in the city, and obviously restaurants were compensating by serving plenty of onions.

In this washroom there were two compartments, one with a Western-style toilet, on which one sat, the other a Chinese-style one. He could never get used to the Western-style toilet—he had even had the one in his home removed and a Chinese toilet installed.

Just as Jia's problem was about to be relieved—splat! He felt a drop of icy water hit the back of his neck. The sudden surprise contracted his large colon and success eluded him. Jia looked toward the ceiling and saw many droplets of water tenuously suspended from a large U-shaped pipe. He was suspicious of the chemical content of those drops. He stood up hastily. He remembered now why he'd made a habit of taking care of this matter at home each morning: this washroom had been in the same condition for quite some time. Why hadn't Plant Services done something about it yet? They'd let that pipe leak for months. All this served only to fuel his anger over his water's being cut off and the long lines waiting for breakfast.

Even though his pressing concern had shrunk back into his lower bowel, he was nevertheless quite aware of its presence in his lower abdomen, and it made him very uncomfortable. The problem had to be relieved. He climbed the stairs to the third-floor toilet. Before he entered he saw that bricks had been placed at the entrance to dam the water covering the floor. There was an ocean behind that dam. The water was too turbid for Jia to guess at its content. This scene explained why the pipes downstairs were dripping "water." He turned and instantly went down to the first floor, to the region "almost exactly like a foreign country." The toilet was locked and there was a sign on it that said: "Toilet under repair—no admittance."

What kind of a day was this going to be? Everything was wrong—eating, drinking, having a bowel movement, urinating.

✎ The Bureau Meeting

"Today's agenda includes the following items:

"(1) The City Party Committee's decision on our bureau's application for funds to build a new block of apartments for high-ranking intellectuals.

"(2) Status report on purchase of site for above-mentioned building.

"(3) The application for building materials from the City Building Committee.

"(4) The application for construction-team contracts.

"(5) The report on cost per square meter of building the above-mentioned block of apartments.

"Now let me give you a report of the City Party Committee's decision on our bureau's application for funds to build a new block of apartments for high-ranking officials. . . .

"The second item concerns the acquisition of land. Under this heading there are several points to discuss:

"(a) The feasibility of acquiring the land.

"(b) The necessity of acquiring the land.

". . . With the concern and support of the Provincial Committee and City Committee of the Chinese Communist Party, some one hundred thousand yuan have been found for construction of the block of apartments. This fund cannot be used for any other purpose."

Jia felt dizzy and nauseated. Only the second item— three more still to go. When would this meeting end?

"(c) The guidelines for selection of land."

But why had the problem of the leaking toilets been allowed to continue for months?

"This problem is very complicated. . . ."

Laughter . . .

Giggles . . .

Laughter again . . .

A final burst of laughter from someone. The laughter was as welcome and as much a relief as the song of the first swallow of spring. But what were they laughing at? Was there something funny in the words of the report they'd just heard? Jia didn't know. Whatever the reason, it was good that someone laughed. He wanted them to laugh more. . . . His eyelids were getting heavy. He felt as if he were floating between two mountains, one of fire and one of ice. He felt pushed from side to side. Two mountains squeezed him and spun him around and around. He was so dizzy he couldn't bear it. He wanted to stop whirling but didn't seem to have enough energy to stop himself. It was similar to when people dream that they must run and yet cannot move a single step. He could do nothing but allow those two mountains to continue spinning him, farther and farther away. The sounds around him seemed absorbed by the substance—was it clouds or snow—that enveloped him. At last he felt absorbed by that substance and dissolved into it. The dissolving was very comfortable.

Jia's head nodded forward, his chin against his chest. His limp body slid soundlessly onto the floor. The last, fleeting impression that passed through his thoughts was that now nothing could disturb him.

>✂ *Seminar for the Working Plan for the Year 2000—Rough Draft*

". . . The Working Plan drafted by the Bureau is, I think, quite comprehensive. The goal of the draft is very clear and the method is very powerful. And it is in accordance with the Four Cardinal Principles, laid down by the Central Committee of the Chinese Communist Party in 1979. I for one am in total agreement with this draft and have no objections at all. I feel we can now proceed according to this draft."

"Bureau Chief Niu, this document is only a draft, which is why we have asked all of you to come here to Beijing to look it over and give your various opinions. You comrades work in the front lines—in the countryside, in the factories; I'm sure you have a lot of practical experience and can offer advice. I hope everyone here will feel free to speak his mind."

"Hm? Ah, right, right. Speak our minds freely . . . Vice–Bureau Chief Mao from our bureau has already expressed many ideas. Everyone, please tell us what you think about this draft."

"Is the representative from X City in Z Province present?"

"Yes, he's present."

"Telegram."

"Thanks."

Oh yes, mountains of documents and oceans of meetings! But these telegrams and telephone calls have gotten out of hand. In the past, telegrams and long-distance calls caused hearts to contract with fear and made bodies tremble, because they were always associated with notice of someone's death. Sending a telegram today is as easy as sending a letter. There are some who even go so far as to say "I kiss you, my darling" in their telegrams. No wonder the price of sending a telegram has gone up. The long-distance telephone rates may go up any day too. But even if the charges for telegrams and long-distance calls doubled, people wouldn't use them any less.

"Xiao Mao, what's the matter?" the man was asking his assistant. "What does the telegram say?"

" 'Bureau Chief Jia Yunshan Died Ten Thirty-five A.M., 21 August 1984. Please Return ASAP!' "

"This will be the death of us! Jia's death will create such upheaval. Our cabinet will have to be reorganized. You can't imagine how hard the Party Committee had to work to organize it last time. The members of the cabinet number only eleven, but they represent all aspects of the CCCCP. There are of course members from the leadership of the Party; from the elderly, middle-aged and younger generations; from workers' unions; from the Communist Youth League; from the Women's Federation; and from outside the Party we have intellectuals, minority and majority nationalities, people from

73

Taiwan, and so on. Because of this diversity, the Bureau could make great progress. And now, my God, we have to reorganize this terribly complicated cabinet."

"But we only have to add a new bureau chief, don't we?"

"No, you don't quite understand yet. The composition of the former cabinet, as I've just described it, evinces a delicate balance. . . ."

"How about Bureau Chief Jia's family? His wife isn't well now. . . ."

"Well, that's because she has borne so many children. Nobody made her do that."

"No one stressed birth control ten years ago. Instead there was a slogan that ran: 'The more people there are, the more enthusiasm there will be and the easier it will be to accomplish more.' And his old mother, who is paralyzed, his son with dementia . . . the Bureau should take care of his family well."

"Would you mind if we stopped talking about these things until our meeting is over? We'd better discuss the draft of our plan first."

"DO you want to take a walk, or would you like to come to my room and share a watermelon with me first?"

"What about the matter of former Bureau Chief Jia? The bureau leader is asking us to go back there and give him our decision."

"All right. Let's talk about it. Just a moment—let me get a toothpick first. Hmph, really poor quality— snapped as soon as I tried to use it. It's only six-fifteen. They're showing a movie in the meeting hall at seven— want to see it?"

"No, I don't."

"You don't? What a pity. It's a restricted movie, not shown to the public. I've heard it's an American movie. There's a kind of movie made abroad that children aren't allowed to see, and I'm not sure whether it's that kind or not. If it should happen to be, we should take this chance to broaden our outlook. And speaking of Bureau Chief Jia, I think we should simply return to the Bureau and report what we decided about Jia's family. Of course, at the same time, we must seriously attend to the meeting here. Comrade Jia was an old comrade who devoted his life to the Revolution, so we must make the best arrangements for his funeral we possibly can. This meeting of the Central Bureau is also very important; it would reflect very well on our bureau if our plan was presented well here. I suggest that one of us go back and the other stay on to attend this meeting. Since you studied the draft of our plan very earnestly, I think you should remain and I'll go back first. What do you think? If you don't agree with me, you can go back instead of me."

"You are the person who should go back first, of course. You are second in position of leadership at the Bureau. I was thinking only a moment ago that now you are the backbone, the main pillar supporting the entire bureau. It's of no consequence to me whether I stay here. My primary concern is that we make good arrangements for the dead man's family."

"Xiao Mao, I can see I was justified in choosing you to be one of the leaders of the Bureau. You have a sharp pair of eyes—you see the issues clearly and analyze them quickly. I'll recommend you for promotion this time, I promise. It's unfair to keep you in the eleventh position in our group—it requires you to do work beneath your talents. All right, then. You stay here. I'll go back as soon as possible. I have many things to deal with. Please ask the service desk to book a plane ticket for me for tomorrow."

"All right."

"Well, then—I'll go to the movie."

"All right."

"And Xiao Mao, one more thing, the speeches we each gave in the meeting don't disagree on any point of principle, do they?"

The Third Meeting of the Funeral Committee

"We discussed the question of Comrade Jia's cinerary casket in the second meeting, and reached agreement on buying a cinerary casket costing one hundred yuan, to be charged to the unit. However, this casket is available only for cadres whose classification is level ten or higher. Comrade Jia was a level eleven, just under the standard line. So we'll have to discuss this matter again. What sort of cinerary casket shall we buy?"

"Why didn't they sell it to us anyway? We paid!"

"It was no use. His classification was lower than what was required."

"What nonsense! Comrade Jia worked all his life for the Revolution, and at the end he can't have a one-hundred-yuan casket!"

"Comrades, be quiet, please! There is one thing I'm afraid you don't know, which I'll explain to you all right now. The hundred-yuan casket is made of *phoebe nanmu* and ornamented with gold wires on the surface. This wood is rare, which is why only the deceased with a rank higher than ten are entitled to a cinerary casket made of *phoebe nanmu*. I don't think this will always be the case, though. The price should come down when the *phoebe nanmu* business is developed."

"What is *phoebe nanmu*?"

"It's a type of camphor wood, grown in Yunnan and Sichuan provinces, very hard and durable."

"Why don't we just concentrate our attention on discussing what kind of cinerary casket we should buy?"

"Damn it! I don't believe that we can't get that casket! Find some way, through a 'back door'—and try to get eight or ten of them, so you and I can reserve two of them for ourselves, just to avoid a problem in the future."

"I'd like one too!"

"You again? You want almost everything. We aren't talking about color TV sets this time, understand?"

"Be quiet, all of you! Do you realize it's now two weeks since Comrade Jia's death? The hospital has been urging us to move the body. Their space is limited, and we can't occupy that bed too long—there's a backlog of corpses at the morgue who have already waited a long time."

"My God, why is it so hot in here?"

"Do they even have to line up to enjoy the morgue?"

"Is there no escape from standing in line? You even have to do so for cremation. Who ever let people have so many babies? Serves us right! It never would have happened if we had heeded Ma Yanchu's advice."

"What about the eighty-yuan casket? What kind of wood is it made of?"

"I don't know."

"What kind of decoration is on it?"

"I don't know."

"Anyway, I think a stainless-steel cinerary casket will be fine."

"We really should move along now. We do have other questions to discuss."

"I said at the beginning of the meeting that we should encourage frugality in arranging a funeral. That doesn't mean we don't respect Bureau Chief Jia. Many old comrades have left wills specifying a simple funeral with no memorial service. Comrade Jia Yunshan didn't leave a statement because he died suddenly, but he would have stated such a wish if he'd had time. I didn't hear what you said a moment ago, but I don't think we can practice perfect egalitarianism. I think we should take the middle. It would be acceptable to buy a sixty-yuan casket."

"I was told that BaBao Shan has no more space for high-ranking cadres' ashes, and a new document states that the ashes of cadres whose rank was lower than ten must be removed by their families."

"Just look at me! I'm streaming with sweat—my clothes are soaked."

"Don't start a rumor. BaBao Shan is very large."

"Please don't interrupt them, you two! Let them get this business settled. Is there really anything to discuss? It makes no difference whether we buy a forty-, sixty- or eighty-yuan casket. You argue here about the cinerary casket, but when the workers in the crematory carelessly take a handful of ashes and give it to you, you won't even know whether the ashes are really Comrade Jia's or not."

"Who is in charge? Are you a member of the funeral committee?"

"Ha—he'll argue furiously, till he's red faced and thick necked, if you don't allow him to join the funeral committee, but he'll refuse you if you do invite him."

"You couldn't call it egalitarianism. We will all die someday. Yes, it was I who insisted on buying the one-hundred-yuan casket last time, and you all agreed with me later, didn't you? I didn't hear any opposition then. He's hardly dead and we're treating him like dirt. We can't let that happen. People would be bitterly disappointed."

"Isn't it because we took part in the revolutionary movement years ago that we enjoy privileges now and at our deaths?"

"What do you mean by that?"

"Oh, listen—revolutionary words again! Our vice–bureau chief can do nothing but quote these scriptures from the time of the Cultural Revolution."

"He didn't learn them in vain, anyway; he's attained the title of vice–bureau chief. He was much more comfortable than we were—he suffered nothing at all during the Cultural Revolution. He didn't share the 'hat' with us, wasn't accused of being a person in power who was taking the capitalist road. He never lived in a 'cowshed' as every capitalist roader was forced to during those years. He has always been considered a loyal revolutionary cadre, both during and after the Cultural Revolution. You shouldn't take it amiss if he's good at the scriptures."

"Come, please! You're straying too far from what we should be discussing now. Egalitarianism or privilege, whatever, we'll discuss those issues later."

"I wonder why they must always argue with each other, on every point."

"I say we'd better buy an eighty-yuan cinerary casket. Fact is, I don't think it makes any difference at all to the country if we spend twenty or thirty yuan more. It's absolutely unnecessary for us to argue, to get red faced and thick necked and waste so much time."

"It makes no difference to me. If I wasn't at this meeting, I'd have to be at another meeting somewhere else. I don't care."

"Say, is that new fishing rod of yours a good one?"

"Of course—it cost more than a hundred yuan. That's more than a *phoebe nanmu* cinerary casket."

"Toss me a cigarette, will you?"

" 'Scrounging' brand, right?"

"Very funny. Here's a public notice from the city government stating that, effective immediately, no one can raise chickens at home. What am I supposed to do with my chickens—I have more than ten! Am I supposed to kill them all at the same time? I can't do that—in this heat, the meat would spoil right away."

"Oh, God! It's so hot I'm nearly dying. We'll never have another Jia Yunshan!"

"Why not be a little generous and share those chickens with someone else?"

"So. Any discussion? We'll buy the eighty-yuan cinerary casket if there is no objection, right? No objections. Consider it decided, then. I left the special meeting in Beijing early to come back here to complete proper arrangements for Comrade Jia's funeral. It's sufficient to say we have fulfilled the responsibility of the revolutionary class toward Comrade Jia. We'll go on to the next item.

"Unfortunately, Comrade Jia's old mother had another attack of apoplexy, brought on by the sudden shock and her overwhelming sadness. The hospital is short of nurses and needs people to help attend her. But under the circumstances, it's very difficult to ask family members to go to her. I think we'd better send several comrades to the hospital to take care of Comrade Jia's mother in shifts. Everyone consider these questions: (1) Do you agree we should send people? (2) If so, how many people should be sent from each department? (3) People who do night work should receive extra pay for this. The standard established in the past is thirty fen per hour, but that is too little now, isn't it? If we increase this amount, how much should we raise it to?"

"We must send people. Who'll take care of Jia's family if we don't?"

"How about two people from each department?"

"I think we should send more than two from each department. People will go in shifts, and the more people we line up to go, the less often each one will have to go. Apoplexy is a chronic sort of disease, a war of attrition. So I think we'd better plan on quite a few people to help. Without extra help, the regular hospital workers will be exhausted."

"Each department should be free to choose who they wish to send. All we have to decide is how many people must be sent; we needn't concern ourselves with specific names et cetera."

"To specify a certain number of people isn't reasonable. Every department has a different number of workers. Some departments have forty-odd people, some have only ten. It wouldn't be fair to the department of ten if it was asked to send the same number of people as the department of over forty."

"But just a minute ago you said that we can't carry out egalitarianism, didn't you?"

"Great—these two are fighting again."

"There's another problem. It's not suitable to send male comrades to care for an old woman, I'm afraid."

"When is this meeting going to end? I'm dying!"

"No, of course we can't send male comrades to the hospital."

"But if we exclude all the men, we won't have many people to send. All the women will have to help."

"We'll have to exclude those with babies."

"We'll also have to exclude all those who themselves have some illness."

"Thirty fen is too little to pay for a night's work. Nowadays workers can earn bonuses, and even peasants can become 'ten-thousand-yuan families'; but our cadres can get no extra income at all. There are many comrades who will count the thirty-fen night-work pay as part of their regular, necessary income to support their families. They won't use that small sum to buy anything extra for themselves to eat. So instead I think we should just give them eggs. For their health's sake, they must at least eat properly."

"Forget that idea. They would save the eggs to take home to their children."

"Or pork braised in brown sauce, then."

"It's useless; they'd save any food you gave them and take it home. Don't restrict them by trying to do their thinking for them—just give them the money and let them spend it as they will."

"Thirty fen is definitely too little. How about fifty fen?"

"Fifty fen! Five yuan would be more like it. But where am I going to find that kind of money? It's clearly stipulated that night-work pay is thirty fen."

"That doesn't matter. Just submit an expense account for 'work/dinner' to the treasurer's office."

"Yes, of course! That's wonderfully clever!"

"Let's see now, maybe we can find a few more loopholes. For example, the monthly bus pass."

"Some people don't need a monthly pass at all, because they don't take the bus."

"But the distance between their homes and the hospital is greater than that between their homes and the office. And after all, it's night duty."

"It isn't much farther though, is it? It's almost the same."

"I wonder why you're so stubborn."

"How about the people who ride their bikes?"

"We could also submit a claim to the unit for the wear and tear on the bikes. They'll be worn out. I think we'd better be as ambiguous as possible with this matter, and not be as explicit as we have been in the past. We'll have to be flexible in looking for ways to get more money. Just look at the ways people in factories and companies find to get extra money. One of my relatives got nearly two hundred yuan from his unit at the end of last year."

"Please don't talk about that. I think I could enjoy making mops. I heard about a farmer who earned 117,000 yuan making mops. The combined salaries of all our vice–bureau chiefs and department heads would add up to less than that farmer's pocket change!"

"It's true that some cadres quit their jobs and open their own private businesses."

"Have you heard of any bureau chiefs or department heads who have done that? After all, we've been educated by the Party for many years now—how could we ever be concerned only about money?"

"It's said that there are model Party members among the individual producers and peddlers, correct? The CCCCP even has a representative assembly of individual producers."

"Maybe you are right in saying that. But some people can be absolutely right no matter what they say—they switch their theories to suit today's policy as well as tomorrow's."

"It seems to me that the unit should pay us a meeting allowance. Attending meetings is a big drain on our physical strength. I can lose half a kilo attending a meeting."

"Comrades, is it all right if we include all these kinds of allowances in our total?"

"No, the people who don't go to the hospital would oppose it."

"What objection could they make? The more you do, the more you get."

"True, but let me give you an example: If you go to the hospital, the people who are left to work in the office would have to finish the work you leave behind. Are you sure they would be doing less work than you? Can you say they wouldn't also be helping Comrade Jia's hospitalized mother?"

"How can you do accounts like this?"

"How can't I do accounts like this?"

"Oh, please, don't argue just for the sake of arguing. Why take it so seriously? Why don't we just count heads in the unit and divide the total allowance evenly?"

"Comrades, on this matter we can afford to be a little vague, but at the same time we must be responsible. We cannot stress money to the neglect of political-ideological work, or vice versa. The first thing is political-ideological work; the second thing is distribution according to work. Work more and get more; work less and get less. Do nothing and get nothing. Can we decide on a standard now?"

"Bureau Chief Niu, it's now twelve-ten. I suggest we have a rest. The weatherman predicted a high of thirty-seven degrees, but it must be hotter than that now. Although we comrades are healthy enough, we can't be certain that this heat won't make someone ill."

"But we haven't reached a decision yet about taking care of Comrade Jia's mother and distributing allowances."

"I say we leave it to you to decide such things, Bureau Chief."

"No, we must develop a democratic style of work."

"But even in a democracy, a leader can make some decisions alone, right?"

"It's not appropriate. Comrade Jia Yunshan has died,

and I am only temporary head of the Bureau. I can't make decisions on my own authority; group leadership would be more suitable."

"It's twelve-twenty now!"

"All right. I'll adjourn the meeting for today. The funeral committee will continue to discuss the matters of taking care of Jia's mother, and allowances, at eight-thirty tomorrow morning."

"These two items should be taken to the Party Committee meeting or the Administrative Department meeting for discussion."

"Now that the Party Committee and the Administrative Department have split, do you know which should be in charge of these two matters?"

"You're wasting your breath! Party Committee or Administrative Department, either way it means more meetings. You can never escape."

"Let's adjourn, agreed?"

"Right. We'll continue at eight-thirty tomorrow morning."

✂ *The First Personnel Assignment Meeting*

"These papers are very detailed. Have you read them? The first section is a general introduction. There are eleven people in the cabinet, including ten Party members with an average age of fifty-six. According to the most recent CCCCP policy, whenever possible, cabinet members should be selected from cadres between the ages of thirty and fifty. This group should not be changed for at least five to eight years. Everyone's record is included: age, education, experience, relatives, political background and experience, experience during the Cultural Revolution—whether a Red Guard, whether the victim of political persecution, any articles written, political attitude—anyway, very detailed."

"Yes, they certainly are. I have read all the personnel records carefully, and some parts of them seem a little different from my memory. Maybe my memory is wrong. Mm, when was Lao Niu elected into the revolutionary cabinet?"

"I can't remember."

"A little earlier than the heads of other bureaus, wasn't he?"

"No, it was just the opposite of the way you remember it. I remember that he was the last to join the cabinet. Then again, maybe he was one of the earliest to declare his position. Oh, my poor brain, it can remember nothing! It must have been injured by the Red Guards' sticks during the Cultural Revolution. If we judged simply on the basis of these papers, everyone would be good enough. It's like trying to choose a wife from photographs. Some people look better in photographs than in life, and with others it's the other way around."

"We have several old comrades here, and they're relatively familiar with these younger cadres. Could you tell us something about each of these people, please?"

"All of them?"

"You don't know them all, do you?"

"This Mao Lu, what unit did he come from?"

"From the General Bureau."

"When?"

"The year before last."

"Why did he change units and come here?"

"His wife works here."

"That means he wasn't here during the Cultural Revolution. Let's check his file to see whether he did well then. . . . Hm, according to his file, he was all right."

"This comrade is only forty-seven years old, one of the last group of graduates before the start of the Cultural Revolution."

"Someone remarked a moment ago that reading these files is like looking for a wife through photos. That comparison is interesting, very interesting."

"We could send someone to his former unit to investigate him."

"It was said that his views on the draft of one of the big programs wasn't in harmony with principles handed down by the higher authorities."

"Was it? Hm . . . I guess that was said."

"Ah, a young man like a newborn calf who doesn't fear the tiger . . . ha."

"Who said that?"

"It was . . . perhaps . . . Oh, I forget who said it. Anyway, someone said it."

"You don't have a very good memory, do you?"

"Everyone, please be more specific and accurate when you express an opinion."

" 'In the later years of the Cultural Revolution, I was released from the "cowshed" I lived in and was sent to cadres' school. I arose at three every morning during the summer, through the rice sowing and harvesting. The sky was still dark, the sun was not up yet. When we went home from the fields at night, it was completely dark. We worked like animals for more than twelve hours a day. I was in charge of supplying rice seedlings. So I shouldered the heavy loads of rice seedlings, and hurried along the low banks of earth between the fields to take the seedlings to those who planted them. The banks were very narrow and hard. The seedlings had just been taken from the cultivating fields, so they dripped water the whole way, and the water made the banks very slippery. So slippery. I'd take one step, and then slip the next step. . . .' "

"Chen Lao, perhaps you'd better . . ."

"Just listen to me! We should have a good beginning as well as a perfect ending. How can we cut head and tail off? Where did I leave off? You see—I can't go on after you interrupt, so I have to go back to the beginning. 'In the later years of the Cultural Revolution, I was released from the "cowshed" I lived in and was sent to cadres' school. I arose at three every morning during the summer, through the rice sowing and harvesting. The sky was still dark, the sun was not up yet. When we went home from the fields at night, it was completely dark. We worked like animals for more than twelve hours a day. I was in charge of supplying rice seedlings. So I shouldered the heavy loads of rice seedlings, and hurried along the low banks of earth between the fields to take the seedlings to those who planted them. The banks were very narrow and hard. The seedlings had just been taken from the cultivating fields, so they dripped water the whole way, and the water made the banks very slippery. So slippery. I'd take one step, and then slip the next step. . . .' "

"But do you have anything to say that is related to the new cabinet?"

"Why won't you let me speak?"

"All right, speak, please."

"You see, again, I'll have to begin all over again because I was interrupted. 'In the later years of the Cultural Revolution . . .' "

"Chen Lao . . ."

"Shhh—you mustn't interrupt him!"

" '. . . Suddenly I fell into the dirty water with an awful splash. I was covered in mud. When we went home that night, I went to the well to wash myself. I used up several basins of water in vain. I was still terribly muddy. Then someone secretly handed me a piece of soap. Can you guess who that was? It was Lao Niu.' "

"That's true, Lao Niu is very respectful of old comrades, and not because he has any special close relation with them. Chen Lao, please go on."

"That's all I wanted to say. I've finished. I simply meant that that was the best possible time to read people's consciences. Had I ever given him any advantage or favor in the past? No, nothing. Before the Cultural Revolution, when Niu was promoted to be vice–bureau chief, I wasn't working in the Bureau yet. Why did he do me this favor? Because of his deep affection for the Party."

"Chen Lao, do you mean that you feel Lao Niu ought to be made bureau chief?"

"Me? No, I don't. I didn't say that! A thing like this should be discussed and decided by all of you."

"Chen Lao, you are wanted on the telephone."

"Oh, certainly . . . You go on, please. I won't be long."

✄

". . . NOW, where did I leave off? The Cultural Revolution? Wasn't that it? Tell me where I left off."

"Well, you said . . . Oh, I'm sorry, Chen Lao, I can't remember. You've said so much."

"That's too bad. I'm always being interrupted when I'm in the middle of speaking. I can't go on without beginning all over again. You see, I can't even finish a speech without interruption, not to mention a meeting—when can you attend a meeting without a hitch? Never! One moment a leader wants you to give a report, the next moment a subordinate asks you to sign a document. It seems that all these details are very urgent, but the meeting itself can be interrupted at any time. Sometimes I've thought I should simply let them cut me into eight pieces: one could be in charge of answering telephones, one in charge of signing documents, one in charge of giving reports to leaders, another in charge of attending meetings. . . . Anyway, back to my original subject . . . Where did I leave off?"

✂ *In the Doctor's Clinic*

"Please try to remember accurately. Before you felt the scorching heat on the skin of your left shin, did you feel anything else?"

"No, nothing special."

"Hm, suppose you just tell me everything you did that day, from morning to night."

"A meeting. I attended a meeting. The meeting of the Personnel Assignment Group. I was on stenography duty. I'm a secretary, so it was natural for me to serve as a stenographer, nothing unusual. But I did feel that it was very difficult to record—they gave speeches, but I couldn't understand what they meant. This kind of thing has never happened to me before. You can check my records if you don't believe me. I was a top student at the university, or I would never have been assigned to such an important department. It was impossible for me to take notes. I began to doubt my ability. Some people who get top scores in school are unqualified to do even the simplest jobs when they graduate. But others who earn lower scores in school are as comfortable as fish in water when they get into the workplace. Oh—I'm sorry, I think I've strayed from the point."

"It doesn't matter. Just tell me whatever you want to say."

"When I found I couldn't take notes any longer, I thought I'd better go out to get some boiled water for the meeting room. I picked up several empty thermoses and stepped into the corridor. I walked around the courtyard for a while—I was a little absentminded. The courtyard is very large, there are several buildings in it, for the many units and departments. I didn't realize I'd reached the back gate of the courtyard until I was greeted by an acquaintance of mine. My God, when I looked at my watch I saw that half an hour had passed! I hurried to fill the thermoses and was very worried that my absence might have held up the meeting. When I went back into the room, the old comrade who had been speaking when I left was still speaking. I listened and realized that his words were exactly the same as the ones he'd been saying when I'd left half an hour before! It was a relief."

———

"Was the meeting over soon after you filled the thermoses with water?"

"No, it was about ten in the morning, and the chairman declared a ten-minute recess. It turned out to be longer than ten minutes, though. There is one comrade who is very good at *qigong*,★ and he practices every day at this time. He works his *qi* around his body very skillfully, and his navel begins to trace an invisible circle, first clockwise, then counterclockwise. The joints of his lower back, in fact his whole body, shake like a deboned pork shaken by a butcher! He repeats the exercise three times, can you imagine that? Just think how long it would take us! You're laughing—is something funny? I know it doesn't involve me or the meeting."

"You went on with the meeting after the break, didn't you?"

"Yes, of course we did. We certainly couldn't finish a meeting like that in one morning. It must last several days, recess for a while, then begin again. Why must it recess for a while? I don't know. I'm only a stenographer. After that break, the comrade who was speaking before the break began again. He started the very same story all over again—in the same words. I felt a little impatient. I'm a bit different from others when I become anxious or impatient. I just can't keep from laughing or rubbing my hands together or shaking my legs. If I can laugh secretly to myself or rub my hands together, that's safe enough, but shaking my legs can cause trouble. This time it certainly did. I knocked a thermos over

★ *Translators' note:* A refined breathing and meditation exercise; *qi* means "vital force."

and it smashed to bits. The boiled water splashed everywhere."

"And it was at this time that you burned your leg?"

"My leg? No, no, my legs are fine—the hot water didn't scald me at all. The thermos fell away from me, not toward me, so the water splashed in the other direction. Then the old comrade stopped. People began to chat about other things—from the smashed thermos to tea, from tea to beer, and from beer to spirits."

"Have you had the burning sensation on your left leg from that time?"

"No, I haven't. This feeling began after I'd attended several meetings."

"When did you first consider seeing a doctor?"

"Well, after people began to look at me strangely. It's enough to make a healthy person think he has a psychosis."

"Have you mentioned this burning sensation to anyone else?"

"No, never."

"And people have begun to say that you've developed a psychosis since then, is that right?"

"Nobody has said that."

"Didn't you just say that someone told you that you have a psychosis?"

"No, that's my impression. I didn't say anything about anyone else saying it. Please check your notes carefully, Doctor. The notes you take must be very accurate; there must be no mistake. Please be careful. It's very important—it can be connected to moral character. You never know when someone might refer to these records to determine whether I have a good or bad character. Some people are so careless in their note taking that they 'lose three and forget four'—they can make a wonderful speech sound like a mess. A speaker could be in terrible trouble if some leaders happened to read the notes of a bad stenographer. I'm therefore meticulous about my work, and that's why I became so nervous as soon as I failed to catch the meaning of what was being said."

"Was there anything in particular that triggered this feeling?"

"Let me give you an example: I like to stand by the window and look outside at noon. There is a stream on the other side of our courtyard wall. It's not remarkable, nothing especially interesting. It doesn't have a willow or a soft grassy bank, and the water isn't clean. But it is a flowing stream, it comes from somewhere and it's going somewhere, it's not just a ditch or a muddy puddle. Like all rivers, it flows from the west to the east. A poet once said, 'People feel sorry for rivers flowing east all their lives,' but it's hard to tell whether people notice the direction of the water when they look at rivers. We always think all the leaves on a tree look alike, but in fact each one is different. We often mistake similar things for identical, when they are actually quite different."

"I'm sorry, but what I want to know is what makes you think people are saying you have a psychosis."

"Perhaps it was because I always stood by the window and watched the stream. As soon as I'd go to the window, the old women would start talking. 'Hey, look—he's looking at the sky again!' Actually I was watching the stream, but they insisted on saying I was watching the

sky. They were wrong, weren't they? It wasn't I who had
a mental disorder! I can no longer see the stream from our
window—a new building blocks the view. Between that
building and the two yellow older buildings, all I can see
is a square patch of brownish dirt, sand and rock. Having
no choice, I happened to raise my head one day and
discovered another square above the buildings, and this
was far more lovely than the ones below. It was blue,
blue—and from time to time clouds floated by. So I began
to watch the sky."

"I don't think you have quite understood my line of
questioning. Well then, tell me, please: Is there any history of mental disorder in your family?"

"No. I've never heard of any. At least there haven't
been any such cases in the last three generations."

"Are you married?"

"No."

"Do you have a girlfriend?"

"No, nothing."

"Have you experienced any psychological trauma in
the past? For example, were you ever disappointed in a
love affair, or refused membership in the Party, or turned
down for a raise in salary, or did your leader ever appear
to have it in for you?"

"No, none of these things has ever happened to me."

"Okay then, let me have a look at you. Eyes forward
. . . Okay, cross your legs. . . . Okay, extend your arms to
the sides and close your eyes. . . . Okay, take off your
socks and lie down on the bed. . . ."

"Is anything abnormal?"

"No, according to my examination I can find nothing
wrong."

"I was afraid you wouldn't find anything. Thank you, Doctor. But why are you writing me a prescription if everything is normal?"

"I'm a doctor, you know. I've examined you, and this consultation has gone on for over an hour, and well, I should, I think, give you something, a prescription at least . . . or can I do anything else?"

"But the medication . . . ?"

"Believe me, it's absolutely without side effects."

>< *Investigation Meeting*
   of the Personnel Assignment Group

"We ought to examine our mistakes, as this meeting should have been held long ago and should have been over long ago. Because of various obstacles, we've been delayed until today. Everyone is aware of today's agenda, right?"

"No."

"Why not, Vice–Bureau Chief Niu? We mailed a notice three days ago."

"Mm . . ."

"What he said is incorrect. We were told about this meeting and its agenda just today, at noon. We were told to attend a meeting at two today in the Bureau, and that the leaders would collect our opinions about the new cabinet. Maybe you left your office before noon to go shopping?"

"That's true, it was announced, and the notice said that we should take the meeting very seriously, and be very honored by the attendance of our comrade leader. Please don't waste time; make your speeches as brief as possible. I'd prefer that you had already discussed and condensed your opinions . . . but the notice was mailed a little too late, so I'm afraid you won't have done this."

"Wrong. We're prepared for this discussion, and all the representatives took part in the preparation meeting. We have a consensus."

"Let's begin the discussion, then."

"Where is Comrade Mao Lu?"

"He hasn't come, has he? We informed him. God, how could he miss such an important meeting?"

"Vice–Bureau Chief Mao told us that he was going to Unit X and Unit N to investigate next year's wood supply."

"We contrive to get hold of many cubic meters of wood each year, and every year we use the same excuse, 'The factory has to move to another location.' We're always such mice about it. That's why we move all the time and why Project X, for example, has grown a long beard. That project was begun fourteen years ago, but we must report to the leaders that it is still unfinished and that we need X additional meters of wood."

"How else could we get wood if we didn't go about it this way?"

"Let's get back to our topic. This is a meeting—we must make the best use of our time."

"It would be nothing if we got even five or six hundred meters of wood this way. There are units that go much further than we do. I joined the Communist Party secretly in 1944, and even broke a leg in the Revolution, but in spite of all this, I'll give you a bit of advice. Don't take it all so seriously; remember even Chairman Mao warned us about that."

"Look here! This isn't a meeting for production arrangements!"

"He always plays the fool, but he never misses the chance to buy a piece of every sort of furniture the Bureau makes from that wood."

"Get on with the meeting."

"A thousand cubic meters is almost nothing. Who doesn't have at least one relative who wants to buy wood? Is there anything you can get without giving something in return for it?"

"What are you shouting for?"

"Get on with the meeting! Please, everyone, stick to the agenda!"

"All right, let me say something first. We promote a cadre not only according to his education certificates but also according to his job performance."

"How can you actually measure job performance? Why don't you show us all how you do it, right now?"

"I have an idea that I haven't fully thought out yet. I wonder if the head of the Ministry's Personnel Department could be the chief of our Bureau."

"It seems to me that the people in the Personnel Assignment Group are stupid eggs."

"You're wrong—I understand it's a very powerful group. Why do you suppose they organized the Personnel Assignment Group? It must be that the Ministry failed to control the Personnel Department. Haven't you heard? They're collaborating to recommend the head of the Personnel Department as our bureau chief."

"Really? Do you know him well?"

"To some degree. This comrade has been perfectly in line with the CCCCP for many years. . . ."

"How many years?"

"Well, since the Third Plenary Session of the Twelfth Meeting of the Central Committee of the Chinese Communist Party, in 1979."

"Comrade Lao Niu, what's your opinion?"

"Ah, well, what he said is certainly one view. . . ."

"I mean, what do you think about the new cabinet?"

"Hm, well, this question should be decided by the leaders in the Ministry. As for my opinion, I'd prefer to consider all sides of this question thoroughly. I think the decision to set up the Personnel Assignment Group is quite correct, but I haven't made my own choice for the new bureau chief yet."

"Any other ideas?"

"No more. Now that the Personnel Assignment Group is established, I hope it makes careful determinations. Of course, no one from any of the 'three categories' can be elected to the new cabinet."

"That's quite right. Every past political movement has produced groups of opportunists. Should we discuss how to distinguish who falls into the 'three categories'?"

"That is set out fully in a document from the CCCCP. Vice–Bureau Chief Niu, you haven't read it, have you? You'd better read it."

"Oh? Ah, yes, yes, certainly I will, as soon as I have time. Xiao Li, don't forget to find a copy for me as soon as we get back."

➤ The Fourth Personnel Assignment Meeting

"Thanks to everyone's efforts, we have finally made a degree of progress. Someone suggested last time that Comrade Mao Lu could be made bureau chief. I had no time before that meeting adjourned to say anything, so I'll speak now. Comrade Mao Lu's job performance is acceptable, and he has had no big political problems in the last years. But he is a little careless in his work and therefore is not qualified to be head of the Bureau, I'm afraid. I think we'd better name another head cadre to assist him. We old comrades have carried out our task only when we have helped a young cadre mount his horse and then also accompanied him on the journey. This way we fulfill our responsibility."

"The fact that he has had no big political problems these past years indicates that he has been good, doesn't it?"

"That was only because the old comrades before him ensured political soundness."

"Today we are face-to-face with the vice-secretary of the City Party Committee, and I must ask for a clear explanation of one thing. Who decided on establishing the Personnel Assignment Group? And why wasn't such an important thing reported to me? It was done without the permission of the City Party Committee or that of the Bureau's Party leaders. What department of the City Party Committee dares to act in this manner? You may go and check."

"Allow me to explain the situation. The decision was made by the Bureau's Party leaders. It was then discussed

at the meeting of the next higher department. We informed you, but you didn't attend. You don't often miss
meetings, do you? We supposed that you weren't well,
and we sent you a document reporting our decision."

"I didn't see it."

"Why do we report everything to him? He isn't a
member of the Party leading group, though he sits above
the Party leading group like an emperor."

"No matter, just humor the old man."

"Chen Lao's speech shows that he has a very deep belief
in the principle of Party spirit; he's an old Party member."

"Don't put it that way, please. No one can disagree if
you put it that way. Each person can speak only for
himself. I can't represent you."

"Nobody has spoken against the policy of the CCCCP,
but it isn't easy to implement. There are those old comrades who contrive to set up a shadow cabinet to rule
from behind the screen. It's true that we suggested orga-
nizing the Personnel Assignment Group, but we had
permission from the City Party Committee. Still, the
thing was difficult to carry out. We received a notice from
your cadres' section that said: 'Without examination and
approval from our cadres' section, the Organization Department cannot send anyone to the Personnel Assignment Group.' So we did nothing and just waited for
further information from you. We didn't know that the
notice was decided by the head of the cadres' section
himself, without the permission of the department head
or the Party leading group, until the head of your section
began pressing us to hurry."

"Comrade Head of cadres' section, I asked you about
this specifically at the meeting of the Organization De-

partment, and you told me you were not opposed, didn't you?"

"Yes, I did."

"Then why did you issue such a notice to the Organization Department without authorization? How could you deviate so far from correct organizational procedures? You've worked in the personnel and organization field for so many years."

"It's a routine organizational procedure and is unnecessary to be reported to leaders. Is there anyone who enters a unit without being checked by the cadres' section? I would be neglecting my responsibilities as a cadre if I didn't proceed this way."

"He was deceived by his own cleverness; he went so far as to investigate the Organization Department."

"How could he control the entire situation and take a seat on the throne of the Bureau if he didn't first control the Organization Department?"

"All officials have crowds of followers behind them."

"It goes without saying. You see, either Chen Lao or the head of the cadres' section has taken great pains to build up his own 'force' in our unit for twenty or thirty years."

"Being an old comrade, I must warn you that I cannot be held responsible for what you do in that way."

"Chen Lao, nobody asked you to be responsible for it. You've often said that you seek nothing and fear nothing. Frankly, I go even further than you do. I'm only an interim figure, why should I worry? I came here only to make a new personnel assignment, and I'll leave as soon as I finish. If anyone wants to try to manipulate the reorganization of the cabinet to suit his own ends, I don't care who he is, I'll prevent him. In our meetings we discuss various names, and then people leave the meetings and immediately begin to talk. People are very sensitive to matters such as personnel assignment, and we must not spread around publicly what is said here. It appears we can keep nothing secret—it's almost as if there is a listening device in our meeting room; by morning our proceedings are public knowledge. Then people begin to interfere in the setting up of the new cabinet. We've just had a long-distance call from Beijing. The caller said that Lao Niu is an honest comrade who in his youth took part in the revolutionary movement. He grew up in the revolutionary ranks. He hasn't been fortunate in getting promotions in the past, and the caller suggests that Lao Niu should be named the new bureau chief. We investigated that call and found that Lao Niu had dispatched one of his followers to Beijing. Evidently Lao Niu had promised him certain rewards and promotions if he is named bureau chief."

"It's true that someone called me regarding Lao Niu. It's not wrong on my part to convey a message from the masses to you, is it? There are many rumors and slanderous statements about the new cabinet. Our comrade leaders should show tolerance toward those who report the rumors. Listen to both sides and you will be enlightened; heed only one side and you will be benighted."

"Absolutely right! I agree with you!"

"You don't need to say that. I'm not one of those who want only flattery from their subordinates."

"You don't know me very well, I can see. I have many shortcomings, but everyone who knows me or who has ever worked with me or been my leader knows that I never flatter anyone. In the past I've often held differing opinions, and I told you about them before I came here as department head. As a Party member I would be neglecting my duty if I didn't criticize what I believe is wrong. Perhaps someone kept my opinions to himself and didn't convey them to you, according to routine procedure, so I'll tell you what I think now. It's too early to say that we have no problem with the cadres in the Bureau. Your conclusion isn't the same as that of the investigation group from the Organization Department. At least I can list a few of the cadres whose political backgrounds aren't clear enough; some have problems relating to the 'three categories.' Please tell me how you can select such cadres for our cabinet after the fall of the Gang of Four."

"Mm, Chen Lao was in charge of compiling that list."

"Oh, Comrade! How can you talk that way? The list of names was compiled by the cadres' section, I knew nothing about it at all."

"Why didn't you explain clearly to Chen Lao? Well, we'll have to discuss that later. Comrade Secretary of the Party Committee, I agree with what you've said, 'Listen to both sides and you will be enlightened; heed only one side and you will be benighted.' We'd better do as the expression instructs. You needn't say that I flatter you."

"Oh no, don't take that so seriously—I didn't mean it that way."

"It embarrassed the vice-secretary of the City Party Committee."

"There is no cadre from any department who dares to quarrel with the secretary of the City Party Committee."

"He just said that he's only an interim figure and fears nothing, didn't he?"

"Rash people fear brutal people; brutal people fear desperate people."

"The vice-secretary has his own plan, or he wouldn't be seriously concerned with this matter. Anyway, this 'interim figure' won't give in. The secretary would get in trouble if he didn't agree. It's impossible for the secretary to exceed his authority and meddle in someone else's affairs. We have to observe the democratic-centralism principle, after all."

"In any case, the problem must be resolved as soon as possible. This crowd of headless dragons cannot go on any longer, or further trouble will result. I can't understand why our leaders acted so weakly in this matter."

"I'd like to conclude this quickly. I'll repeat what I said at the first Personnel Assignment meeting. I said: The City Party Committee ordered us to set up the new cabinet as soon as possible. But has that speeded matters up? On the contrary, the situation has become more and more complicated. It is not a case of scheming behind the scenes any longer but of conspiracy on the stage. I've read some books by Han Feizi, and although my analogy is to an emperor's political trickery, I think you will understand my point."

"How do we deal with the relation between one finger and the other nine, between the part and the whole? We often forget how to do this in our daily work. We shouldn't think the future is so dark and describe the problem as so terrible. I don't want to put any political hat on anyone's head, but I am a Party member, and I have to point out that you haven't been objective or calm enough; you've compared our revolutionary work to Han Feizi's political trickery. How could you say such things? Today the vice-secretary of the City Party Committee attends our meeting, and the support from the chief of the Organization Department . . ."

"No, no, don't make an example of me. You did it in 1959 and I was labeled a rightist opportunist then."

"What you've said is far from the point. I had nothing to do with your label."

"Of course, you praised me at the time: 'See what close friends Comrade A and Comrade B are, they can talk about everything with each other. We should build up such close friendships between comrades.' Yes, yes, you were quite right, a friend of mine was accused of being a rightist opportunist, and because he and I were so very close, the leaders tried to force me to expose him. And because I failed to do so, I was labeled a rightist opportunist."

"Enough. You've pushed him, and he's kicked you. But in the end the new cabinet will not reflect any one person's desires."

"Please pay attention now. The Personnel Assignment Group has done a great deal of work and has produced a plan that is in accordance with the policies of the CCCCP, and not according to any one person's will. Now we ask the Personnel Assignment Group to tell us its decision regarding Bureau personnel."

"Comrade Mao Lu will be in the head position of the cabinet. Comrade Niu will be . . ."

"Right—that's good."

"No, I disagree. It means more centralization of power."

"Thank heaven and earth! At last it's over!"

"Don't celebrate yet—I'm afraid we're not finished."

"What? Centralization? I'm surprised to hear you say this now. Didn't we eliminate the pernicious influence of big democracy during the Cultural Revolution? Anyone who disagrees with the plan can complain to higher authorities. But remember, you must go ahead with this plan while you're waiting to hear from those higher authorities. You may not put a stop to it unless the higher authorities make a new ruling that rescinds the previous plan."

"Vice-Secretary, do you have any instructions?"

"No, I don't. I'm only a guest at this meeting."

"I hereby declare this meeting adjourned."

⊱ *July of the Following Year,*
 at the Working Conference of the Bureau

"Listed below are the items we will report to the new cabinet:

"(1) The City Party Committee's decision on our bureau's application for funds to build a new block of apartments for high-ranking intellectuals.

"(2) Status report on purchase of site for above-mentioned building.

"(3) The application for building materials from the City Building Committee.

"(4) The application for construction-team contracts.

"(5) The report on cost per square meter of building the above-mentioned block of apartments.

"(6) Progress report on the discussion by each branch committee of the Party and all workers in the Bureau concerning the circumstantial evidence from the local police station in District A brought by person X exposing person Z for robbing a member of D democratic party, the object of the United Front, the well-known Mr. E's antiques, jadeware, gold, silver and jewelry during the Cultural Revolution, and person Z's accusation that person X framed him."

Translated by Deborah J. Leonard
and Zhang Andong

✕ Professor Meng
Abroad

PROFESSOR Meng ran out of the elevator in such a
hurry that he even forgot to thank the operator.

This was such an elegant hotel, one that preserved the
traditional standards of a grand hotel from the past.
Instead of being automatic, the elevators were operated by uniformed men wearing white gloves; the tables
in the dining room were set with candles; the lintels
and wainscoting were decorated with seventeenth- and
eighteenth-century designs. . . . The atmosphere of
quiet grace and refinement made Professor Meng feel all
the more like a savage for not saying thank you to the
operator.

But he didn't dare stop or even slow down; he lengthened his stride and dashed through the hotel's classic
lobby. All the other members of the delegation were
already in the minibus; he was the last one again. He
knew what sort of looks Miss Ding was giving him
through the minibus window, but if he didn't go to the
toilet before they set off, when would he find another?

It was very difficult to find toilets in X, and it was even
more difficult to find a public toilet where you didn't have

to pay. Maybe people in X had especially large bladders. Professor Meng admired this capacity very much. Of course he knew it was impossible to see anyone's bladder, but he couldn't keep his eyes from straying to the lower abdomen of everyone he passed.

Even if you did find a public toilet there was still the danger of losing your life. In these places you frequently ran into muggers and murderers who might bludgeon you to death and steal all your money. Professor Meng didn't have a penny in his pocket; all he had was his passport. All the money he and the other delegates had was safe in Miss Ding's hands. Apart from all the valuable knowledge in his stomach, he didn't have anything that was worth bludgeoning him for. But would anyone believe that? He could easily be mistaken for a provincial landowner; his new suit was made of high-quality wool, although it was decidedly unfashionable. It would be safer to have someone come with him and keep watch outside the door. But Professor Meng hated to burden anyone else with his own personal matters, in spite of the Central Committee's policy that intellectuals should be esteemed and treated as valuable. After decades of being told that intellectuals must remold their ideology and become more like workers and peasants, more proletarian, Professor Meng now found it difficult to ask for preferential treatment. Besides, how could he trouble other people to help him do something as unpleasant as go to the toilet? Even cats are discreet enough to hide their excrement—shouldn't humans be at least as circumspect?

After getting into the minibus late again, he didn't dare meet the eyes of the other delegates; he confusedly nodded in their general direction with a foolish smile on his face.

"All right, now everyone's here. We can go," he heard Miss Ding say to the guide in flawless X-ese.

He didn't turn his head, but he could feel her icy stare on his back, and he pulled his trench coat a little closer around him.

Oh, damn. He had to go to the toilet again. Since he left China his complaint had worsened. When he was at home he didn't have to go to the toilet this frequently. He could control himself for more than two hours at a time. There was no doubt about it.

Out of control, everything was getting out of control. And the more nervous he became, the more he had to go to the toilet. But he'd have to put up with it for now.

He couldn't ask for the minibus to stop, and make everyone wait while he searched the world for a toilet. Besides, they were now on a highway; where could they stop? This led him to marvel again at the bladder capacity of the people here. He had heard that they drove for hours on the highways without stopping. Could it be that there was something special about the way their bodies were constructed?

This morning the group was to visit the ruins of a medieval castle. The picturesqueness of the crumbling ancient wall inspired one's imagination.

Miss Ding smiled at last; it was as if a plastic mask had been removed from her face. As she stood at one point along the ruined wall she lifted her chin and narrowed her eyes, her long, soft hair stirring in the autumn wind. It lifted the hem of her cream-colored trench coat, revealing the milky-white wool skirt she wore underneath. How elegant she was! Miss Ding was the pride of this entire delegation made up of fusty old bookworms. She was like a crane amid a brood of chickens.

And she never seemed to go to the toilet.

For some time now, Professor Meng had been unable to enjoy the medieval architecture; he had an urgent need to go to the toilet. He had searched around the castle walls, but he couldn't find a public toilet that was free of charge. Reluctant to abandon his search, he continued to look. He never wanted to ask Miss Ding for money if there was any possible way around it, because she always insisted on a detailed explanation of why he needed the money. It was humiliating. It suddenly occurred to him that in such a refined and civilized place, there just could not be something as crude and vulgar as a toilet. This time he didn't have any choice but to request the money from Miss Ding. It was upsetting. He hesitated, not having the courage to go up to her. He could only stand apart from the others and wait for Miss Ding to return to reality from her poetic dreamland.

She finally turned from the ruins with a heavy sigh, and Professor Meng approached her with a smile that could be taken as either modest or ingratiating. With great difficulty he said, "Please give me some money, Miss Ding. I—I need to wash my hands." He mumbled, half swallowing the words.

Miss Ding stared at him for a full minute as she calculated how much money she had already given him for toilets. They had been traveling for ten days and Professor Meng had asked for money on average twice a day. He had spent forty units of this country's currency already. Miss Ding checked her watch. It wasn't even ten-thirty yet—perhaps he would ask for money more than twice today. Ironically enough, Professor Meng was an insulin expert; it was a shame he hadn't studied polyuria. He could help diabetics, but he couldn't do anything for polyurics.

Why hadn't the doctor discovered this problem when Professor Meng had his physical examination before making this trip abroad? He wouldn't have been allowed to come if it had been known. He really was a burden. When they went from G to E the whole delegation nearly missed the plane because he was going to the toilet. Everyone else had already boarded the plane and was thinking that perhaps Professor Meng had fallen into the toilet and couldn't climb out. As she hurried back and forth in front of everyone, worrying about him, Miss Ding's face had grown red and damp with perspiration.

She looked at the loose muscles in Professor Meng's body, and they seemed to her like bread soaked in milk. If you pinched his flesh, surely liquid would come through the pores. How could he not be polyuric?

She dug some change out of her purse and said, "Why don't you use the public convenience?"

"There isn't one here," Professor Meng said apologetically, as if it were his fault.

"The whole delegation's allowance for tipping is not going to be enough to pay for you to 'wash your hands,' " Miss Ding said, suppressing her anger.

Oh, no—what Miss Ding said was impossible; her calculations must be mistaken, Professor Meng thought. This sort of talk perplexed him and made him uneasy. It would be absolutely impossible for him to infringe on others' interests in that way. He had to clear up this confusion. "According to the rules, each person is allowed ten yuan per day for tipping, and six people make that a total of sixty yuan. It's impossible for me to have spent all that. I haven't even spent my own allowance yet." He felt his face and ears flushing. He was ashamed to have to speak like that, ashamed of his polyuria, and ashamed to have to explain his reasons for needing the money. . . . He felt entirely alone, abandoned in this strange place. He, who was regarded with esteem by his superiors and with affection by his students, whose every need was taken care of by his wife and children, and who was highly respected by his colleagues in other countries, was reduced to having to ask for a pittance, like a beggar. He couldn't even go to the toilet in peace without undergoing this cross-examination and having to meet that expression on Miss Ding's face that cut him to the quick. He was homesick. He would have boarded a plane for home immediately if it had been possible, just to avoid ever having to see that hard plastic face of Miss Ding's again.

Miss Ding frowned. She already felt overworked by this delegation of six people and now this Professor Meng was making matters worse. The expression on her face was in stark contrast with the soft hair on her shoulders, her cream-colored trench coat, milky-white skirt and exquisitely thin high heels.

"Do you think the money is used only for this purpose?" Miss Ding carefully avoided using the word "toilet." "Don't we also have to tip the hotel waiters? And the porters? And to rent the luggage carts? . . . I know everyone is sick of me and calls me a witch. Do you think I enjoy listening to everybody explaining the reasons why they want tipping money? Maybe you think I skimp and save so that I can use the spare cash myself. Okay, here. That's enough. You take care of your business right now, and you'd better hurry."

Professor Meng, in too much of a rush to think over what Miss Ding had said, had the feeling that he had unfairly offended yet another person. As he walked hurriedly away, he was careful to keep his legs together, trying his best to tighten all the muscles in his lower abdomen, while desperately looking for a toilet. He didn't know where to find one. Looking around, he realized he was in the middle of nowhere. He nearly despaired. He wanted to cry. A vivid and embarrassing image flashed into his mind. That would certainly make headlines!

"Wait a moment!" Miss Ding called from behind him. She ran to the minibus and said to the driver, "Would you kindly take this gentleman to a washroom, sir?"

Translated by Deborah J. Leonard
and Zhang Andong

✄ What's Wrong with Him?

THE cigarette stub burned through his trousers, cotton underwear and underpants, scorching his thigh. Only then did Hu Lichuan realize that he'd dropped his wallet into the spittoon and stuffed his lit cigarette into his trouser pocket. There was nothing wrong with his eyesight. But it wasn't his eyes that told him this, it was his thigh. He had been staring blankly. Now he darted a glance at the spittoon. Strange, his wallet had disappeared.

In other words, he now didn't have a cent on him.

Damn it! No one could say for sure when the plane would leave. Hu Lichuan had no money for a meal or a hotel room.

The time of his flight was clearly marked on his ticket: ten o'clock. Now it was already twelve.

Why couldn't they leave on time? He had gone to the office to ask. If he hadn't done that he might not have dropped his wallet into the spittoon and stuffed his half-smoked cigarette into his pocket.

As Long As Nothing Happens, Nothing Will

Between ten and twelve he had made the rounds of the waiting room five times. Had scanned the faces and luggage of well over a hundred passengers. Had speculated what illness each might have. This had become a hobby of his, a habit, a way of killing time. What else was there for a doctor off duty to do?

He believed that a thorough medical checkup would reveal something wrong with everyone. But they'd pay no attention until their illness became terminal. Would even die (unless shot) in a trance, not knowing what they were dying of.

Those faces, well over a hundred of them, were hard to differentiate. Each seemed half listening, half watchful, half asleep, half awake. Even a bomb thrown by a terrorist couldn't arouse them from their apathy.

Their hand luggage looked practically identical too: the same black plastic handbags; the same red, white and blue nylon bags; the same brown plastic briefcases; the same net bags filled with oranges or bananas bought in G—oranges fifty fen a pound cheaper than those in F, bananas one yuan cheaper.

Well over a hundred faces, not one registering impatience, worry, doubt or anger over the plane's delay. As if they were in no hurry to go anywhere.

Perhaps they'd been standing for so long that now that they had a seat they meant to stay put forever. Melted, glued and worn down by that seat. The world held nothing but that seat—no workers, peasants, traders, students or soldiers; no eating, drinking, shitting, pissing or sleeping.

What mattered was that oranges were fifty fen a pound cheaper than in F, bananas one yuan cheaper. But since the plane was late, the fruit was senselessly, innocently rotting. The bittersweet smell of rotting bananas and the bitter-sour smell of rotten oranges pervaded the air. No one noticed that the bargain buys were slowly deteriorating. Everyone was still too busy congratulating himself on having found such bargains.

If these hundred–odd people fell ill, thought Hu, no doubt they could all contract only the same disease. The idea made him suddenly tense. He feared the earth would open its huge mouth and swallow the people sitting there into its bottomless maw. He longed to escape, to tread on air and fly up to the sky. To go on flying forever and ever.

Finally, on his sixth round, he found a face able to register discontent. A woman's face. "Shouldn't we go to the office to ask why the plane is so late?" she asked him. Whom else could she ask? It was like a horse accosting a horse, a lion a lion, or a deer a deer. They needed no introduction. And no interpreter either, just as when dogs, cats, birds or tigers communicate.

The duty officer said, "I don't answer questions like that."

Why ask such a question, the duty officer wondered. Can the hundred-odd people in the waiting room answer my question: Why are you so apathetic, so fatalistic? Why don't you ask why the plane can't leave on time?

If it couldn't leave on time, that was that. Just like those apathetic people sitting there fatalistically with no sign of impatience, worry, doubt or anger.

Hu had to sit down again. He felt as if he were sitting in an old well. It was deep, and its smooth sheer sides had no jutting stones to clutch at.

That was when he dropped his wallet into the spittoon and stuffed his cigarette stub into his pocket.

He had no idea who could have taken his wallet. He made another round of the waiting room. He couldn't imagine any of these seemingly half-listening, half-watchful, half-asleep, half-awake people spotting his wallet in the spittoon and having the sense to take it.

Who could it be? He really couldn't tell, couldn't guess. It was like the old legends about frogs, lizards, stones or plants transforming themselves into human beings and performing superhuman feats, then changing back again into frogs, lizards, stones or plants.

✂ 2

It was complicated yet simple.

Simple because in checkups at the district and municipal hospitals Ding Xiaoli's hymen proved to be intact.

This showed that on her wedding night her husband hadn't consummated the marriage. In that case she was still valuable.

In that case she had changed from a loose woman into a model of chastity.

In that case her husband had withdrawn from the court his appeal for a divorce.

In that case he loved her again. "I've never loved anyone else as much as you," he swore. That is how characters in modern stories and films and on TV often talk. Previously such talk was confined to foreign stories, films and TV, but now they talk that way in China too.

In that case the man must be impotent, or else an ignoramus. . . .

In that case his medical diploma wasn't worth a damn.
In that case . . .
Was she Ding Xiaoli or a hymen?
Was it she he wanted to marry, or her hymen?
Was it she he loved, or her hymen?
Ding Xiaoli felt confused.

It was very cold. She hitched up the padded coat with which she had been covered. It was heavy, not having been washed for more than twenty years, since the hospital first opened, and the dust on it must have weighed several pounds. Ding Xiaoli dozed off and dreamed that she had grown larger, thinner. Turned into a huge hymen so thin it rustled in the wind. She ought to take a scalpel and cut it into bits two centimeters square to sell to women whose husbands were of no use, to guarantee that at one puff they would break. She could make a fortune that way, and the divorce rate would drop. The Committee to Uphold Morality would surely award those women prize money or certificates, as memorial archways were no longer erected in praise of chastity.

Her sister-in-law wrote that Ding Xiaoli's father had stopped working. All day he sang snatches of opera, tickled the soles of his wife's feet or peeked through windows to watch married couples in bed. Ding Xiaoli didn't believe it. Didn't want to believe it.

OLD Man Ding had hired a tractor from Ding Dali's private transport company. Ding Dali, his son, was Xiaoli's older brother.

The tractor, farting all the way, headed toward the purchasing station. Farting all the way—quite something. Ding Dali, the transport company manager, wore a Western suit of synthetic material, gray with red pin-stripes.

Didn't such a harvest, such cotton, call for putting on a show?

Farmers had grown rich.

Ding Dali had meant to charge his old man half-price, but his wife wouldn't hear of it: "With a twenty-five-percent discount you're already running at a hell of a loss." Old Man Ding, cradled in his cotton bolls, was figuring how much he'd make after deducting expenses. He couldn't use an abacus, could only read the figures on banknotes. But he could work out his accounts correctly. And his greatest enjoyment in life was figuring out how much money he'd made. Not even his wedding night could compare with this.

Someone was sleeping under an old, half-withered scholartree on a slope by the road. Sleeping on his back with his mouth open. A bloated fly crawled up and down his lips, flying off lazily only when he snored loudly, to circle close to his face before settling again.

The rumbling tractor set the earth vibrating and woke this sleeper. He sat up and leaned blankly against the old tree. His blue jacket was unbuttoned, his bright red sport shirt rolled up to his armpits, exposing his lean stomach and protruding belly button. But he seemed thoroughly relaxed.

Wiping his face with the palm of one hand, he grinned at the jolting tractor—it must be overfed, the way it was farting; must have something very wrong with it.

The tractor jolted away, trailing black smoke behind it like a cuttlefish its ink.

The man raised his head to stare at the sky. Stared till

his head drooped. His chin touched his chest and he fell asleep again.

OLD Man Ding got off the long-distance bus and headed home, singing an aria from the Hebei opera *Qin Xuemei Mourns Her Dead Husband.* He felt good. Could he have felt as cheerful as this before Liberation?

He'd burned all his cotton. What could anyone do about it? Hands clasped behind his back, he plodded along on his stumpy legs and proudly wagged his head.

First-rate cotton. No doubt about that. The flames had shot up, so hot that he sweated, so bright that they dazzled him.

Old Man Ding begrudged spending money on an inn. It was very warm in the cotton. Who could have known that all of a sudden it would rain? The cotton, covered with plastic, wasn't wet. He lavished more care on it than on his own son and daughter. But the autumn rain chilled him to the bone and brought on an attack of rheumatism.

He begrudged eating out, just munched baked wheat bread.

Who could have known that he'd have to wait three days?

If he moved into an inn on the fourth day and went to an eating house . . . Old Man Ding figured that it wasn't worth it. Better just stick it out.

Men who had arrived after him had already had their cotton weighed and had left.

Old Man Ding was very shrewd. He discovered that a gift of two bottles of sorghum liquor enabled you to jump the line. Four bottles changed third-grade cotton into second-grade, and second-grade into first.

The men selling cotton heard his joints creak and advised him: "Give them liquor and they'll weigh yours first, so that you can go home."

"Who made this rule?"

Old Man Ding was a fool to ask such a question in the purchasing station. In reply they told him, "We'll weigh yours when we have time." They didn't refuse to weigh it, but they'd weigh it when they had time.

"Shit! Do I have to beg you?"

After a few days of this, some devil got into him. He set fire to his cotton. Burned it up in the purchasing station. That staggered the county town. People crowded around so closely to watch the fun that not a drop of water could trickle through. "Go and watch 'em burning cotton, come on!" More and more onlookers flocked around, even rushing in from outside the town gate. The head of the militia yelled: "Make way, make way for the hoses!" But the crowd hemming in the fire refused to budge. The secretaries of the County Committee took turns cranking the telephone until they upset its stand.

By this time Old Man Ding was on his way home, singing a snatch of opera in a falsetto shriller than widows bewailing the death of their husbands.

No longer did he need to worry about putting up at an inn or eating out. No one, whether in inns, eating houses or the purchasing station, would be able to get him in his clutches again—he was liberated, free. No one would try to take advantage of him. He hadn't lost out, hadn't let anyone cheat him. His mind was at rest.

Just then the fellow sleeping under the old scholartree awoke. He sat up again and leaned against the tree. At intervals—the time it takes to smoke half a pipe—he threw back his head and bellowed at the sky. His bellow carried two *li*. His eyes were sharp, his muscles taut. His resonant yet hoarse voice sounded vital but lifeless, animated but wretched, genial but desolate. As if he had boundless energy but had exhausted his strength.

Next year, thought Old Man Ding, there'll be a drought.

WHAT complicated matters was that Ding Xiaoli wanted the divorce.

That being so, she'd had a checkup. Like a pig fresh out of a slaughterhouse after examination, with a blue chop stamped on its big white rump.

That being so, she'd been probed and prodded time and again. After all that probing and prodding, even a freshly picked peach would turn rotten. Even now, no matter where she was, she felt she was still lying, legs wide apart, on the gynecologist's table. Whoever passed by had to look in. Let one look and you had to let ninety-nine others look. Ding Xiaoli couldn't refuse, as this was the simplest, most scientific, most convincing method of reaching a verdict.

That being so, more and more people were growing suspicious of her.

That being so, what could she say to her people at home? Especially since her father no longer did any work, spending all his time singing opera, tickling the soles of his wife's feet, peering in through neighbors' windows to watch married couples in bed.

After such a hullabaloo, what could a woman do but ask for a divorce. If she didn't she'd be too unworthy of her hymen.

✕ *3*

They should have fought it out long ago. The earlier the better. Frequent quarrels are better than none.

Some psychoanalysts advocate catharsis. Or call it relieving yourself. If they'd quarreled as soon as the young carpenter moved into this hostel, and quarreled again every week, their present relationship might be much better. Other psychoanalysts advocate repression. If they'd quarreled as soon as he'd moved in and quarreled again every week, that might have made it increasingly hard for them to lead normal, rational lives.

The reason for their quarrel was very simple.

After spending more than thirty hours in the operating room and keeping the patient under observation, Hou Yufeng needed rest. Needed to recoup his energy for the next operation, or to concentrate on some reading material.

The carpenter needed to make furniture for his cronies. Now he was making some for himself. In furniture shops the price of a suite of not bad-looking but gimcrack furniture had already gone up to eighteen hundred yuan. He couldn't compare with those jobbing carpenters who easily earned five or six hundred a month. If the administration hadn't coaxed him with favors—all his tools, nails, hinges, timber, glue, paint and varnish came from the office—he'd have set up on his own long before.

The carpenter worked away day after day, year after year.

Ke-chi, ke-chi, he sawed away at Hou Yufeng's bones.

Ping-ping-ping, he chiseled into Hou Yufeng's skull.

Shala-shala, his sandpaper grated on Hou Yufeng's nerves until they were frayed, torn to rags.

Cha-cha-cha-cha, his plane took shavings from Hou Yufeng's flesh.

"Can't sleep?" said the carpenter. "Well, you can't be sleepy, then."

Eight times Hou Yufeng had asked the Party secretary to let him move somewhere else. And eight times the Party secretary had called the administration.

"How can we move him? There are too many such cases. We know more about it than you do," was the answer.

"Why not house all those in the same line of work together?" the secretary suggested.

"They'd still have the problem of night shifts on different days. Or they'd refuse to move from the third floor to the second, or from a room facing south to one facing north; or they'd object to each other. . . ."

True. Stood to reason.

"Well, then . . . What's the solution?"

"There isn't any."

The Party secretary refused to believe that any problem was insoluble. Especially since their hospital took ideological work so seriously. After those in charge of political work at all levels had tried to make the young carpenter see reason, he told them, "Go on, report me to the Party committee. I'm not a Party member. I've no intention of ever joining the Party. So don't give me that talk—it's no use.

"What do you mean by 'consideration for others'? What have I done to him, eh? Just tell me that."

The Party heads stared blankly at each other. After all, what had the young carpenter done to Hou?

"Can't sleep? He can take sleeping pills. Think I don't know that? Quit bluffing. Just ask anyone: Since when has insomnia counted as an illness? All intellectuals are persnickety. Who's he, dammit, to dictate to *me*?"

It's true, insomnia isn't an illness. But by degrees the mere thought or mention of sleep made Hou's eyes blaze viciously.

He couldn't understand, just couldn't see why he had to stay in that room. He loathed it so much he would have liked to smash it to bits, yet he had to go back to it meekly every night.

Was someone whipping him along? No. Was someone tugging him? No. Was a young wife as fair as flowers and jade waiting for him inside? No. Then why was he unable to leave this place he loathed? What was this pressure on him? Or what was the inducement?

He thought of various ways to escape this pressure.

He might marry the physician next door. She'd surely be willing. For the problem of sleeplessness had spread like the plague through this hostel for single people, or rather this bowl of mixed stew. That would cure not only his headache but hers too. Yes, this bowl of mixed stew could be rearranged. Tripe with tripe, preserved eggs with preserved eggs, smoked fish with smoked fish, duck braised in soy sauce with duck braised in soy sauce. No need to split them all up. But wouldn't that mean that the administration would have to produce more housing? If it could, he needn't marry. Who'd dare marry a woman like her?

What's Wrong with Him?

At a meeting of the Provincial Scientists' Association the newly elected chairman failed to show up; he had been mentally deranged for years. Someone else made his thank-you speech for him. "Comrades, thank you all for electing me as chairman. No one knows better than me how lacking I am in education, knowledge and capabilities to fulfill my task. Yet from now on I shall devote myself entirely to raising my ideological, political and vocational standards in order to carry out the task you have entrusted to me. I shall bend my back to this task till my dying day. . . ."

Before this speech had even ended, the physician from next door called out from the auditorium, "Since he's been ill for so long that he couldn't come, someone obviously wrote this speech for him in advance. Let me ask: How could he know in advance that he would be elected? And if he's mentally deranged, how could he write such a well-organized speech? . . ."

The newly elected chairman's psychosis was quickly forgotten as talk of the woman physician's neurosis swept through the town. To marry a neurotic woman like that would just be asking for trouble.

Or he could tie a straw rope around his neck and go downtown and put himself up for auction. He'd cry, "Hey! I'm ready to marry anyone, never mind how old or young. She can be blind or lame, can hiccup, fart, talk in her sleep. Nationality and sex don't matter. I don't mind a lesbian, just as long as I'm given a room."

That was bound to work. Nowadays plenty of well-paid, highly qualified women with rooms couldn't find themselves a husband. And he wasn't just anybody, a tall, good-looking, well-qualified surgeon like him. If only he weren't in such a hurry to leave this dump, he could have had the pick of the bunch.

But no, that wouldn't work. Before he had sold himself off he'd have been arrested on a charge of disturbing public order.

In fact Hou Yufeng was afraid of getting married. Afraid of milk bottles, diapers, shopping for vegetables and carrying gas cylinders. Afraid of the responsibility. Actually he was highly responsible. Suppose a good woman free to do as she pleased became his wife and started worrying because there was no effective medicine for infantile eczema, because yogurt contained colon bacilli, or because preserved fruit carried hepatitis germs, which might infect the child. Suppose she wore herself out looking for a back door into a kindergarten, or had to mind the child and cook supper as soon as she came back from work, unable to afford a maid. What sort of husband would that make him? If society couldn't provide a woman with the minimal facilities and security, if he had any conscience at all, he shouldn't drag someone free to do as she pleased into this bitter sea. Women who worked with their brains as well as their hands always aged and turned white prematurely.

Or he could simply take an axe and chop down this building and burn it up. Then he and the young carpenter would have to part, whether they liked it or not. . . . This way was the most terrible, yet the most tempting. Since he could conceive of it, he might one day do it. Who could guarantee that he would remain rational? There is no clear demarcation between lunatics and normal people, just as there is little difference between digitalis used as a drug and as a poison.

AS it happened, the carpenter's plane knocked Hou Yufeng's forehead. At once blood spurted out. Fine. How pleasing! Hou had longed for this day. It seemed as if all his frustration, all the misfortunes that had dogged his family for generations were pouring out with that blood.

His great-grandfather had passed the imperial examinations in the Qing Dynasty.

His grandfather had been head of a middle school.

His father was a minor functionary in a government office.

Generation after generation. How to shit, fart, sleep with women, walk, talk, laugh, act in an official capacity or go to court . . . every action had to be carefully considered. They had to reflect: What will people say? What will they think? What will the consequences be? They lived out their lives in fear and trembling, as if walking on thin ice.

Still, his great-grandfather and grandfather, like Ah Q,★ derived a little mental equilibrium from the theory that to be a scholar is to be one of the elite—like slapping your own face to make it swell in an effort to look imposing. In fact they were no better than pet cats or dogs. Didn't rich men keep "scholars" as protégés? When they were in a good mood they would stroke you. When they were in a bad mood they would kick you and throw

---

★ *Translator's note:* Hero of Lu Xun's *The True Story of Ah Q*. Oppressed and humiliated, he worked out a way of winning specious "moral victories" to restore his self-respect.

you out. Protégés had to comply with their master's whims. But at least they were given the acceptable title "scholar." Treated like dogs but not called dogs.

After the policy was to "unite with, educate and re-mold" intellectuals, you were bluntly told you were a dog. All dogs have tails. What for? To wag or tuck between their legs. Wag your tail, dog. Tuck your tail between your legs, dog.

Blood was still streaming from Hou's forehead. He heard it singing, "Kill him—kill him!" That didn't scare him in the least. He clenched his fists and lunged at the young carpenter. Pummeled him like a boxer practicing on a sandbag. Punch, punch, punch—a steady rain of blows.

This punch for Great-grandfather.

This punch for Grandfather.

This punch for Father.

This punch for himself.

This punch for all dogs the world over.

He felt great. His blood was still singing, "Kill him—kill him!"

He felt relieved. He had seen the light.

That night Hou slept exceptionally soundly.

✂ 4

Hu Lichuan was catapulted out. He heard the twanging of a bow fluffing cotton.

Thud! He fell flat on the ground. For a second, before his coccyx started hurting, the cement floor in midsummer felt cold as ice.

At first he had no idea where he was. Where had he

come from? Where was he going? What was he doing here?

Apparently he had been considering whether or not to write yet another curriculum vitae. Didn't the Personnel Department have complete files on everyone? You might have forgotten how when you were five you stole pears from your neighbors' tree. Your dad's two false teeth, were they gold or platinum? How many carats? What did they weigh? Or were they stainless steel? When your dad sold soybean milk he watered it down every day. . . . All these details were recorded in your file. Still, you had to fill up endless forms giving all your antecedents. Those earlier ones might have been eaten by someone who mistook them for garlic pancakes. They must have been savory.

How did he come to be lying in the road?

A big stone in the middle of the road was secretly laughing at him. It hadn't been there before, he was sure of that. It must have erupted from the earth.

Old creatures had prematurely lost sight in their third eye, which enabled them to see the world as three-dimensional.

Just then his radio receiver bleeped. "Dr. Hu Lichuan, Dr. Hu Lichuan. Please come straight to the ward."

Ah, yes. He sped to the hospital. That beeper was a foreign gadget. But it had a limited range and you couldn't communicate with it. So Hu Lichuan had no idea which of his patients needed him or what the emergency was.

All that happened on earth was chancy.

By chance he'd foreseen an emergency tonight and kept his beeper on.

And by chance it was working, so he could hear it distinctly.

By chance he had a bike.

By chance his bike hadn't been smashed.

By chance he lived not far from the hospital.

By chance his patient hadn't yet been sent—as usually happened—to the mortuary.

"SHALL I burn more, Dad?"

"Go on," said Old Huang. The Huangs had pots of money. Banknotes and foreign-exchange certificates. His son earned at least a thousand yuan a month, and he himself could make three hundred.

They had bought pretty much all there was to be had in China, apart from official titles.

What was so special about official titles? All they meant was a free car, an apartment, a telephone and special privileges, or good jobs for relatives and friends. With money you could buy all those things too.

Good jobs meant living well or going abroad. His son was a good enough cook to go abroad. Several cooks from roast-duck restaurants and the Beijing Hotel had gone.

Another ten-yuan note was set alight. Old Huang kept his money in his trouser pocket. It felt moist and smelled of sweat. These last two days he'd been so frantic that the sweat had poured off him.

Small flames from the banknotes flickered on the green grass, making it hiss with pain, its small blades shrinking back.

Old Huang didn't mind spending money. To get housing he'd given a big color TV set that cost eighteen hundred yuan. Wasn't his grandson worth a color TV?

The tiny flames could light up only Old Huang's hands and the lowered faces of father and son.

In the flickering light the wrinkles on Old Huang's hands seemed like so many gaping mouths filled with the dust that had flown up from the countless shoes he had cobbled. With his long, brown, horny fingernails he'd gripped hundreds of thousands of iron nails to mend shoes. He very rarely bent a nail. One blow with his hammer and, straight as a flagpole, the nail drove into the rubber, cloth or leather upper.

Cobbling, like writing stories, is an art calling for perception. A man with the right perception can't go too wrong. He must sense, for instance, just how hard to hammer and how to coordinate the long, brown, horny nails of his right thumb and forefinger.

Who says fingernails have no consciousness? Old Huang's were clutching a wad of notes as if tugging a towrope steadily upstream. He was towing a boat past rapids, a boat with his grandson in it.

His indomitable expression was that of a man ready to lay down his life. Lit up by a flicker from below, the muscles of his normally kindly face had tensed. And the blood racing turbulently through his veins was making them bulge and twitch.

Behind them, out of the light, was the boundless immensity of the night sky and that mysterious building called a hospital. What made it mysterious to Old Huang was that dead men carried in there might come back to life, while living men who went in there might die. It was

as enigmatic as a mysterious shrine. The light in the
building too was like the oil lamp in front of the shrine,
shining neither faintly nor brightly. Now the life of his
only grandson was flickering with that light.

"Go and have a look," Old Huang ordered his son.

Once more his son went to peer through the window
of the ward.

Old Huang's elbows and knees twisted and turned on
the grass, as if this place galled him so much that he could
find no comfortable position. His lips quivering, he invoked the gods one by one and kowtowed to the ghosts of
those hounded to death, vowing to reward them if his
prayer was granted.

"Dad!" his son exclaimed.

Old Huang leaped up and rushed to the concrete windowsill. On his elbows and knees were patches stained
green from the grass, as on some stylish foreign sports
jacket.

The doctors and nurses who a moment before had been
milling around now stood with their arms by their sides.
All but one, who was still massaging his grandson's little
chest as if pumping a bike.

Press harder, you! Old Huang's nails clawed the palms
of his hands. If only he could massage the child himself.

Don't, don't! Don't press too hard, you'll hurt the
child, he thought.

It was no use, no use. . . .

The Huang family line was going to die out here. What
sins had he committed? None. Not even Qin Kui and Yan
Song, who had murdered loyal officials, had had their
lines wiped out. Did Old Man Heaven show favor to
those in high positions?

———

Spirits of heaven and earth, ghosts great and small who rode on clouds or white smoke, he'd invoked the lot of them, prayed to them in good faith, and they'd accepted a hundred ten-yuan notes—he'd seen that with his own eyes. The white ashes of those banknotes, fluttering and whirling, had disappeared without a trace, in no time.

A big color TV could be exchanged for an apartment.

He'd prayed to the goddess of fertility to send them if not a son at least a daughter. Now, even spirits and ghosts didn't work. Just ate up your offerings for nothing.

Old Huang couldn't stand it, dared not watch any longer. His heels thudded back to the ground. He was panting, his knees limp. After standing on tiptoe for so long he had cramps in his legs. He propped himself up against the wall, that concrete wall which provided no warmth or comfort.

"Dad," his son called again.

Old Huang gripped the windowsill again, straining to stand on tiptoe.

All he could see was that someone else had come in. A tall, thin, tottering figure. The fluorescent lamp made his white face look sallow.

Another beanstalk, Old Huang thought. Over twenty years had passed since the "three hard years," yet all these doctors and nurses still looked half starved. No wonder they couldn't cure the child—they seemed at their last gasp themselves.

This one was a doctor, a good one—he knew that.

Old Huang knew most of the doctors and nurses here. He had worked at his stand by the hospital gate for more than twenty years. Generation after generation of doctors and nurses had taken him shoes to repair. He did such a thorough job that, as far as making money went, he was a fool. But he felt this gave him face. At least in this neighborhood his reputation was high.

Luckily everyone wanted a pair of shoes that would last at least a lifetime, if not longer. A crooked heel could be replaced, a worn-out front sole could be patched, a broken strap could be lengthened, a vamp that had come loose could be sewn back into place. Living standards had gone up. Not all China's billion people wore leather shoes, but if five hundred million of them did, cobblers would do a roaring trade.

SEND the body to the mortuary?

Generally speaking, if oxygen was cut off for more than three minutes the case was hopeless. And the child's heart had stopped beating eleven minutes before.

Five years old. Maybe it was for the best.

There was no hope. None. His dilated pupils no longer reacted to light.

Suppose they did an autopsy. There might still be one chance in a thousand.

"Prepare for a thoracic operation." Hu Lichuan told the nurses to swab the child's chest with tincture of iodine while he scrubbed and had a gown and gloves put on.

Rap, rap, rap! Old Huang knocked so hard on the window that it rattled as if in an earthquake. He grazed his knuckles without even noticing.

"Doctor, Doctor, all our ancestors are kowtowing to you."

It was too dark outside for anyone inside to see out. The heads of Old Huang and his son were level with the window, as if someone had put two heads on the sill.

To Hu Lichuan they seemed ghostly. "Draw the curtain, quick," he ordered.

"DAD, am I seeing things?" whispered Old Huang's son. "Why does that doctor look . . ." He couldn't believe that the child was out of danger, but dared not say so outright. He'd learned as a boy that old people tabooed ill-omened talk, as if this were a way to avert disaster. How could they carry on without fooling themselves like this?

Could you duck out of trouble's way? He was more progressive than the last generation. He disapproved of their negative approach and believed in being realistic. If the boy was really done for, he'd decided, they'd have another child. Even though he'd already been demoted two grades and reprimanded in his Party branch for having two children. The second was a son, though; that was the main thing.

He'd always been law-abiding, wanting only to do a good job and get by comfortably. Life wasn't easy. He had no high ambitions. How else could a man like him have joined the Party? The Party, like a Peking opera with all types of different roles, needed some members willing to sweat their guts out. But at the time he joined, the Party hadn't ruled that you could have only one child. So how could he have foreseen that he'd be reprimanded for having two? Had that rule been added on now? He didn't know. The constitution had been revised many times. It didn't seem to have changed much, and yet there had been changes. Directives, clauses, theories and the general gist kept milling about in his brain.

It was his own fault for being a man. As a man he had to marry and have a son.

Since he'd had his pay docked and been reprimanded, things had grown clearer in his mind. Those old codgers all had five, six, seven, eight children. By the time they'd had enough and couldn't get a hard-on anymore, he wasn't allowed even two. Wasn't that always the way? When the first comers had done all they wanted, bagged all the pickings they wanted, they clamped down on the latecomers. The ox-thief isn't arrested, only the fellow who untied the ox.

So he had given up his job in a state-owned hotel. Gone to work in the jointly operated Gold Dragon Hotel. In no time his pay went up fourfold. He'd long since made up for being demoted two grades. As for Party discipline . . . they had no Party meetings in the Gold Dragon Hotel.

OLD Huang and his son saw eye to eye on this. But Old Huang was in more of a panic. "Stop talking rubbish," he bellowed at his son, to boost his own morale. He'd heard they had a special room in the hospital for dead people.

Old Huang tried to avert his eyes from the dark. But it was very hard.

A dark green, blood red, gray-black figure flitted behind his son. Old Huang felt as if the fine hairs on his body had suddenly shot up a foot and swept across his back. He was rather hard of hearing, but now his ears seemed as sharp as those of their cat. And like the cat's ears they were twitching in all directions. He suddenly became as spry as a cat, ready to leap away at any moment.

HEY didn't tear his hair, rip his clothes, beat his chest, stamp his foot, slap his head or redden his eyes by drinking sorghum liquor. . . . He simply shuttled to and fro at the foot of the wall like a frightened ox or mule just caught and corralled, circling around and around inside the fence.

"Heavens, I'm a beast, not a man." The words came from his guts, belly and kidneys, heart, liver and lungs. It wasn't Hey speaking. Hey had no face to speak or show remorse, let alone see daylight or the sun, or face other people.

Some small trees by the hospital wall thrashed his face with their branches. It didn't hurt. His face was covered with lumpy warts, large and small, like clusters of ripe grapes.

With a grunt Hey flopped to the ground like a sackful of grain. The palms of his hands, and his elbows and knees felt sore and tender. The grass and trees here seemed like a bay. After the broken bottles, empty cans, waste paper and plastic bags that had been chucked out of the hospital were tired of whirling in the wind, they cast anchor here. Hey too lay down here on his back. It was as though the smashed pupils and whites of his eyes had been replaced by frantic eyes staring fixedly at the night sky. There was no moon tonight. He couldn't stand the sun but longed for its shadow.

I'm a beast, he thought. For years he had been conscious of a furry tail attached to his backside. Whether sniffing leaves or grass he could always smell garlic sausage, pig's head and sorghum liquor. He couldn't help turning now to take a bite of grass and chew it, chew it. Sure enough, it tasted of mashed garlic and cucumber.

The first time Hey's vigorous daughter, as tall as he was, threw herself naked at him, he not only thought his wife had come back to life but even smelled in the girl's naked flesh the reek of his wife's cunt. Only wild beasts or cattle could reek like that. And only wild beasts or cattle could smell that reek. Living with someone like his wife would turn anyone into a beast.

In terror Hey had beaten his daughter up. She had no idea why. She was a half-wit, a simpleton. Old Man Heaven, why didn't you change her flesh like her brain into a mass of bean curd. That would have saved her. Fuck you, Old Man Heaven.

All day long his daughter cried out, hooted with laughter or flung about restlessly, flaring her nostrils like a cow in heat. Those nostrils quivered and sniffed, and finally, at night, she would throw herself on Hey.

At that time he wasn't called "Hey" yet.

There was no special reason for his fearful filth, his revolting life. It had all started with those warts like purple grapes on his face.

What woman could love or kiss such a face? Could share a pillow with it?

He hated all women. At the sight of him they squealed in such a disgusting way. They were trash. Yet he couldn't help longing to trample on their lewd, despicable flesh.

If they squealed too disgustingly he would turn upon them till his face sent them flying in all directions.

Finally he picked up a madwoman no one wanted. Picked her up.

In those days she was passed like a ball from the hands of an ex-convict to those of a thief, then to those of a hooligan. . . . Could any woman who wasn't cracked have married them? They didn't lust after her just because they were ex-convicts, thieves or hooligans, like people deprived of their political rights and left to wither away. They lusted after her because they thought her much cleaner than those other trashy women.

She wasn't too crazy then. She'd sit quietly on the doorstep, smiling foolishly at passersby. Or mutter to herself in the shade, shifting as the sunlight shifted. If it was a sunless, rainy day she'd lean out of the window to count the raindrops dripping from the eaves, reaching five and then starting all over again.

Only at night did you realize she was crazy. He didn't know how the ex-convicts, thieves and hooligans had coped with her then.

In the dark, stark-naked, her hair all tousled, she would suddenly, silently clamp herself to him. Then he felt she wasn't a woman but a ghost who needed to suck out his manhood to come back to life. When day broke, his face was the color of earth, as if he had just crawled out of a grave, and he would sit cross-legged on the bed watching her closely as she lay sound asleep. She had a dissolute face. Her lips, her cheeks and the bags under her eyes were puffy and shiny. The hairs of her long eyebrows stood up as if they felt the cold. There were dark circles around her eyes, her skin was lusterless, chapped, covered with red spots. . . . As he watched her it dawned on him: She'd let those brutes pervert her. That was what had driven her mad. So she was done for. Once you took that road there was no turning back.

She conceived. What did a man with a pushcart know about eugenics. How was he to know that someone insane was not fit to have children?

After the child was born she went back to that riffraff, like a wild cat with no need for a home. Beating her was no use. . . . Then suddenly she died.

Beating was no use. . . . Now it was his daughter's turn.

They were all mad, Hey thought, his whole family. He felt as if someone had kicked him in the belly, kicked from his viscera and vitals a strange cry—a sob, a groan or a laugh?

Hey couldn't say whether he pitied his daughter or pitied himself. He couldn't bear being tormented, yet he took her when she threw herself at him. She reminded him of his own problem as a young man—no one would marry her or share her bed and pillow.

Beasts, they were a pack of beasts, Hey thought. It wasn't clear to him whether the child she had was his daughter or his granddaughter.

"My child by my dad," his daughter crowed to everyone she met as she held the baby. Simpletons have no sense of shame, they're lucky that way.

She told everyone she met. But his Party secretary didn't know. No one in the hospital knew. It's hard to find anyone to mind the mortuary. It's a badly paid job and an unlucky one.

But no one ever spoke to him. The orderlies who brought bodies from the wards and the accountants who paid him called him "Hey."

Hey was not afraid of stiffs. They couldn't see even if they wanted to. And they didn't call him "Hey." They were more likable than people in the street who didn't know his story. At the thought of the day when he too would lie in the mortuary, dead to the world, Hey licked his lips in satisfaction. This was all he had to look forward to. The thought of it cooled his blood. Made it stop bubbling as it raced through his veins.

The mortuary was Hey's heaven. He should go back there. Wasn't it after midnight? Most patients due to die popped off at this time. Hey got up and lurched toward the hospital. Suddenly he saw two figures below a window. As he turned to go a different way his feet crunched a glass bottle.

Old Huang's taut nerves seemed to snap as the bottle smashed. With a long pent-up groan he clutched at his son and ran.

Some windows upstairs started rattling. Someone asked in dismay, "What happened?"

✄ 5

12·2·19—

The wind blowing through the broken windowpane soon cooled the steaming rice porridge. Sitting on benches like those used by scissors-grinders, they lapped up the warmth from their bowls as fast as they could.

What was wrong with Hou Yufeng? He wasn't eating but instead was rapping the side of his porcelain bowl with a stainless-steel spoon and singing. Singing at the top of his voice. All the others lapping up porridge in the canteen listened, smiling. They knew the song. It was one everybody had to sing in the Cultural Revolution, but he had changed the words.

"Three old dishes
Have to be eaten
Morning and evening.★
Three old dishes
Hard to stomach,
It isn't easy to eat them for a year.
We must take these three old dishes
As a test set by the Party.
Each has got to be eaten
Before going to work.
Make a good job of modernization,
A good job of modernization."

First the others pointed knowingly at the bandage on his head; then when they saw him singing so raptly they felt free to discuss his recent abnormal behavior.

12·4·19—

Toward noon a patient with a head wound was brought to the emergency room. Dr. Chen decided to send him to the operating room. I called several times for the elevator, but it refused to stop on the first floor. It just shuttled between the basement and the second and third floors.

Nowadays we say "Time is money." We talk about "the third wave" and "the main trend." Even peddlers of nylon stockings believe in systematization, cybernetics and "information theory." Yet here, where time is a matter of life and death, it's really shameful the way we procrastinate.

After a few minutes the patient's limbs had grown

★ *Translator's note:* This is a takeoff of a song exhorting everyone to read, morning and evening, three articles by Chairman Mao.

---

cold. I couldn't feel his pulse. If not for the bottle and tube attached to him, I'd really have tried to carry him up, bed and all, to the operating room.

I watched blankly as the numbers over the elevator door lit up and went out, turning from green to black. Now the basement number stayed green. I rushed frantically down to intercept the elevator.

"Why don't you stop at the first floor?"

"Can't you see it's time to send lunch to the wards?" the elevator operator said.

The elevator was crammed with nurses changing shifts, as well as a cart of food.

"I have an emergency case on the first floor. He has to go to the fourth floor at once for an operation."

"At once? Okay, as soon as I've sent up lunch."

"That won't do!"

"Didn't you say 'at once'? That means we can wait three months."

I saw his point. When the elevator for delivering food to the wards had broken down, the hospital had promised to have it repaired at once. Now, three months later, it was still out of order.

"This elevator goes up and down delivering drugs, instruments, food carts and people still alive and kicking. What if your emergency case is infectious or dies in the elevator?"

A head wound isn't infectious, but while waiting for the elevator the patient had died. That evening, when I was starting home after writing a report on his death, I saw that broken-down elevator, with its big face the color of bean curd, cold and impassive. I went over and savagely kicked its big face, kicked my leather shoe apart and fractured my toes. But I felt fine. Better than I'd felt for a long, long time.

When the patient in Bed 4 eats, his food often goes down his windpipe. I discovered that when he came in as an emergency case five days ago he had a respirator inserted. Because this was bungled it paralyzed the right side of his vocal chords and made it impossible for him to swallow properly. I criticized the nurse who had been on duty that day. She said the lighting in the ward was so poor she hadn't been able to see the oral cavity clearly.

12·7·19—

The dispensary is short of antiseptics and is rationing the wards. But we need antiseptics for our patients. I had to send a nurse to different wards to borrow saline solution, then had to dilute it to the required strength myself. We borrowed just enough for today. Gangrene is setting in and antiseptics are essential—what shall I do tomorrow?

12·8·19—

At suppertime the patient in Bed 17 made a scene, because of the high price charged. For one yuan, eighty fen of steamed chicken all he got was one chicken leg. I envy people who can fly into a temper. In all other jobs they can slack off or pilfer tools. But not doctors and nurses. When someone's life is in your hands how can you be so irresponsible?

12·9·19—

The physician in charge of Ward 2 was beaten up yesterday by a patient's family. The patient had rheumatic heart disease, was incurable and died of cardiac failure. I don't know too much about this physician. She always looks exhausted, her voice is hoarse, and she generally buys the cheapest dish in the canteen.

It's too bad, a woman getting beaten up like that. Today I saw her in the elevator, limping, her face bruised and swollen. I nodded to her to show my sympathy. She walked past staring straight ahead as if she hadn't seen me.

12·10·19—

Just after seven the lab telephoned to say all tests would have to be carried out before nine.

I hoped nothing would crop up that evening.

But after twelve a patient's heart started palpitating—170 a minute—and I needed to know the potassium ion content of his blood before taking emergency measures.

At 12:20 I sent in a blood specimen. By 1:00 A.M. no result had come back. This test usually takes twenty minutes. I called the lab. "Comrade, this is an urgent case."

"What's urgent about testing for potassium ions?" he asked.

When I insisted he said, "The machine hasn't warmed up yet." Well, maybe it hadn't.

Urged again, he said, "We can't compare with abroad. They have that multifunctional equipment which in just a few minutes can tell you everything about a blood specimen, including the potassium, sodium and chlorine ion content. If you're in such a hurry, send your specimen to America to be tested."

I was really ready to kowtow to them!

The result didn't come till 2:20, and by then there'd been a change in the patient's condition. I needed a clinical radiograph at once but couldn't find any radiologist on duty.

Our hospital recruits relatives of staff members. Half of our staff are the children of the other half. Criticize one and you're criticizing his parents. Behind your back he'll run to the superintendent or Party secretary to catalog all your faults—and you won't even know.

12·13·19—

Dr. Chen told me to draw up an application for research funds for next year. He also gave me some tips.

"All right, I understand. I'll make a request for two years."

"That won't do, you must put in more projects, big ones. Don't come to me asking for money because you've run out halfway through."

"I can make it out for five years, but that's hardly appropriate. We need to research the most advanced branches of science. After two years they'll probably be out of date."

"Then apply year by year."

"And if we're not ready on time and they come to investigate, what shall we say?"

"No one's ever investigated. Even if they do, those inspectors don't know the first thing about it. Oh yes, you must make allowances for inflation and changes in the rate of foreign exchange. Some of the equipment will have to be imported."

". . . ?"

"We have no idea when this plan will be approved. By

the time it is, the money it costs now to buy five test tubes may only be enough for two."

"I don't work at a currency exchange. How do I know how much prices are going to rise?"

"Aren't you old enough not to need me to tell you?"

12·15·19—

Tomorrow Dr. Chen is going to England as part of an academic exchange. He thrust a visiting card at me, pointing out the titles on it, including "Professor." To judge from his record of service and qualifications he certainly deserves to be made a professor. In fact it's ten years overdue. Recognition at long last was most gratifying to him.

"Congratulations," I said.

"What's gotten into you? The hospital lent me this title and I'll have to borrow it. Going abroad on an exchange like this you need a suitable academic status. When I get back I'll return it."

"Oh . . ."

He smiled. "The personnel department wants me to take a research student, too."

According to regulations a chief physician shouldn't train research students, but for years Dr. Chen has been given that job.

"Who?"

"Ding Xiaoli's husband. But this time I flatly refused."

"Why?"

"If a qualified doctor doesn't even know whether or not he's perforated his wife's hymen, and goes the day after his wedding to appeal for a divorce on the grounds that she wasn't a virgin, is he fit to do research?"

12·16·19—

Today I was on duty in the outpatient department. One patient in a cap inscribed "We Workers Have Strength" barged into my consulting room before his number was called. I asked him to wait his turn.

"Do you know X?" he asked.

I thought and said, "I've seen him on TV."

"I'm his driver."

"Well, I haven't seen you on TV."

"Don't you believe me?"

"No, it's not that. But I think . . ."

"What do you mean, you think? You dare doubt my word? Is this how you treat our heads of state?"

"What are you getting at?"

"Don't you realize that holding me up means holding up one of our heads of state, holding up important affairs of our Party and the country? Think of the consequences. Are you willing to take the responsibility? You'd better examine me right away. If you don't, I'll go and find your boss. Then you'll still have to see me first. Don't give me that talk about implementing the policy on intellectuals. I'll let you see whose say counts." He rattled all this off in one breath. Must have had big lungs to hold his breath so long. And he had good manners. He didn't once raise his voice.

The Party secretary came in and said, "Special circumstances—make an exception for him."

12·18·19—

My ward has just admitted a case of corn cancer, the manager of some foreign trade company. He was escorted here by more than a hundred people: twenty-one assistant managers, nineteen section heads and assistant heads of the personnel department, thirteen administrative section heads and assistant heads, and the heads, secretaries and drivers of the companies under him, as well as his wife, sons, daughters-in-law, daughters and sons-in-law.

Since our corridors are narrow, the Party secretary and the senior assistant manager of his company headed two files of people coming in. I was waiting respectfully on the third floor by the elevator, ready to give the patient a preliminary checkup.

In front of me stood the Party secretary of the surgery department and the seventeenth assistant head of his company's finance section.

The seventeenth assistant section head asked, "Can corn cancer be completely cured by an operation?"

"We can tell only after the operation, and when we've seen how he responds to treatment. Of course, for a special case like your manager's we shall do our very best. . . . But because our hospital is short of foreign currency, our equipment, instruments and drugs aren't first-rate. We've imported some laser equipment but can't take delivery until we've paid another 250,000 yuan. If your company will be so generous as to help us solve this problem, that will be a fine thing for the people of this city."

"I don't see any big problem there. I can report to our director. It's only right that we do this for the people of this city. . . ."

"We can ask our superintendent to operate. He's one of the best surgeons in the whole country. This operation will not only cure his corn cancer but prevent all further likelihood of cancer."

12·19·19—

Dr. Yu also wants to take a second job and teach in the nursing college. Today he brought me his application to sign.

On the left he'd listed his expenditures: rent, water, electricity, gas, transportation, clothes, food, school fees, house repairs and money spent on finding back-door connections. On the right he'd written his income: seventy-five yuan.

What sort of application do you call that?

"I don't approve," I said. We have sixty to seventy beds in our ward and only three resident physicians. If two of them go off to take additional jobs, how can we manage? Brain work isn't like manual labor, with an eight-hour working day. We have to use our off-duty time to bring our medical knowledge up to date. Even if it's only to find out whether there's any new antibiotic better than penicillin.

"All the department heads have agreed," Yu insisted. "I'll go and talk to them."

"I can't balance my accounts—won't you do something about it? If you have time to tackle our department heads, why not get the minister of finance to promote me two grades?" Dr. Yu tore up his application form and threw it in my face, then fell to the floor, frothing at the mouth in a fit of epilepsy.

12·20·19—

Today was payday. Apart from my salary of ninety-eight yuan, I got paid for twenty night shifts. One yuan a night, making twenty yuan—fine. After work I went to the Xinhua bookstore to buy the English-Chinese medical dictionary I'd wanted for a long time.

After leaving the bookstore I went to see the head of X Middle School. We had examined one of his math teachers and found he had lupus erythematosus. The hospital to which he had been assigned wasn't able to diagnose it correctly. So he'd come at his own expense to our hospital and we'd charged more than he could afford. According to him his school wouldn't reimburse him because he looked so "fit and ruddy." His wife had had to go sell her blood to clear their debt.

When I explained this to the head of the school and showed him the results of our different tests, he agreed to get in touch with the other hospital to see about reimbursing the teacher and transferring him to our hospital for treatment.

Praise be!

12·21·19—

The hospital has instructed every department to discuss and decide the annual awarding of prizes.

Dr. Chen said, "We have nine nurses in our department, so each can get a prize. As model worker, model in family planning, most exemplary family, model Party member, trade union activist, outstanding Youth Leaguer et cetera. We won't include any doctors. As for the prizes for regular attendance, they can all be recommended."

"I've no objection to anything else, but how can we recommend them for no absenteeism? They've all asked for sick leave."

"Only because they're worn out from working

overtime. Have you reckoned how much overtime they put in? It adds up to more than their sick leave, yet did the hospital pay them? The prize for regular attendance comes to a whole twenty yuan."

This afternoon Dr. Chen urged me to go to a lecture in the medical college.

I said, "I haven't written our ward's annual report yet, and the higher-ups are asking for it."

"Just make a copy of last year's."

"Last year's was copied from the year before. And that had been copied from three and four years before. . . . Copy it again this year?"

"Of course."

"Suppose they find out?"

"Come off it. You think they read them?"

Dr. Chen is really great. My admiration and love for him keep growing.

12·22·19—

On the night shift our head nurse fainted. At the time she was extracting the impacted stool of the director of the foreign trade company. It fell with a thud into the enamel bedpan. It didn't smell offensive, more like ginseng pills that had been stored a long time.

When I measured her blood pressure it was 60–70 over 40–50. I raised her eyelids: the whites of her eyes were dead white. It was simply anemia. Just over fifty yuan a month, and her son, who has hepatitis, needs special nourishment. More than twenty night shifts a month—it would be strange if she didn't have anemia.

All the nurses in our department are anemic. The only

exceptions transferred long ago to the office, the typists' pool or the lab. They had pull. Others got jobs as receptionists in big hotels. What nurse doesn't know enough English to pass the oral test? I heard that last year when technical secondary schools were recruiting students, only one in the whole city listed nursing as her first choice. Who wants to be a nurse? It's hard, tiring work, badly paid, with a low social status.

I had the head nurse helped to the nurses' rest room and gave her a 500-cc glucose transfusion. At once her blood vessels sputtered. It was so long since they'd had such good nourishment.

After the transfusion she went back to her patient. "He's in critical condition," she said. "Can't neglect him."

The next morning, when the patient's condition was stable, his family wanted to see him. The head nurse stopped them.

"Who do you think you are?" demanded the manager's son. "What's special about you? Don't you just empty bedpans? What right have you to stop me?"

"The patient has just gone to sleep. You'd be risking your father's health, maybe his life," I explained. "In any case, these aren't visiting hours."

"Who are you?"

"The doctor in charge of this ward."

"Who's that creature to stop his family from seeing him?"

"That's no way to talk. You ask who she is. I can tell you. But don't call her a 'creature.' She's a nurse, I'm a doctor. Your father, in our care, is gradually recovering."

The head nurse tugged at my gown. "Don't argue with him. We can't afford to offend them. Our hospital's still hoping they'll help us out with 250,000 yuan."

At the end of our shift I told the head nurse to take her son the oranges left over from when some foreign visitors were entertained. I couldn't understand why she looked so resentful. I'd meant well. I'd never seen such fine oranges in the market.

Yes, those oranges were really extraordinary—not like oranges at all.

1·4·19—

A friend sent me some useful reference material from an international conference, and I took it to the library to be photocopied. I was annoyed by all the fingerprints on it—where had they come from? When I sniffed it, it smelled peculiar.

The librarian refused to copy it. "There's no one else here, and I'm too busy," she said.

"Didn't you recently increase your staff to six? How come there's no one else here?"

"Three of them are at college for a TV course, two are at night school working for diplomas. With diplomas they can be promoted and get a raise."

"Does a diploma mean higher pay? I studied eight years at the medical college and another two years in the United States, but where has it gotten me?"

"So those five new librarians never show up."

"Nowadays all people with pull find some cushy job that gives them time to attend to their own business. They leave the work to others. So in our library all the work's left to an old woman like me."

She's only in her forties—why call herself an old woman?

As I wondered about this I saw countless hands removing their own wrinkles to put on her forehead, pulling out their white hair to stick on her head, as if sticking in needles, and pulling out her black hair to plant on their own heads. They swapped their discolored, half-decayed teeth for her white, regular ones, and their crooked spines for her straight one. . . . In a flash she grew old. Really old. Aged so fast. Then those other countless forms with their countless hands faded away. How could I have the heart to add to her work load?

"I'll do it myself. If I break the machine I'll pay for it. Okay?"

When I'd studied in a medical school in San Francisco, each department had had a photocopier like this.

"How could you afford it? You could sell yourself and still not raise enough money to buy a machine like that."

Then I felt that a hook had gotten me by my trouser belt and was hoisting me into the air. I seemed to hear someone saying, "Hold the steelyard a bit higher."

Someone else said, "The market price is ten fen for ten catties. However high you raise it you can only get an extra three ounces at most."

I looked again at the photocopier and saw it was different from the ones I'd used: it had a magnifier. Each character of the text appeared as big as a house, each fiber of the paper as thick as a tree, each fingerprint like a winding mountain track. I crawled in and out of each room of the houses, climbed up and down each tree, and felt tiny as an ant. I labored disconsolately up each mountain track to each peak, all with magnificent views. Just as

I wanted to feast my eyes on the landscape, a howling wind sprang up. The earth spun around and my eyes misted over. By the time I had hurtled down and opened my eyes, I found myself back by the copying machine. When I came to my senses I realized that I was really light as a bun.

1·7·19—

The administration sent me to the airport to meet Professor Hodgkins, since I'd gotten to know him while studying in San Francisco.

The plane arrived at dusk.

The taxi drove off through the dusk toward the hotel where he would be staying.

The concrete road was gray. The pavements were gray, as narrow as an old belt curled up at the edges. The soil by the pavements was gray. The pebbles in it were gray. The concrete telegraph posts were gray. The buildings by the road were gray; even the people's faces, smiling or grave, were gray.

Professor Hodgkins was staying in a five-star hotel. When you went in, you felt you were in New York or Paris.

Soft music sounded from each wall, ceiling and cranny. The bedroom was tastefully furnished, the bedding even folded just as in hotels abroad. On the bedside table was a convenient phone console. Professor Hodgkins lost no time in calling his wife in San Francisco to announce his safe arrival. In the bathroom were a first-rate tub, liquid soap and everything else men or women guests might require. In the dining room, where Western meals were served, there were soft lights on the tables. The waiters

spoke fluent English and were polite. In this atmosphere I
felt no longer like a bun but like a distinguished chief
surgeon, someone with a slavish respect for everything
foreign.

If one-tenth of the capital investment, efficiency and
smiling service of this hotel were given to any other unit,
it would feel transported to heaven. Not that I propose
giving our hospital a share.

After seeing Professor Hodgkins settled in, I met
Young Liang, a former nurse in our outpatient department, on the first floor. She looked much healthier now,
and very smart too, in her trim, close-fitting woolen
uniform.

She greeted me eagerly and invited me to the bar to
have a chat.

"Thank you, thank you. Some other time. It's too late
today, no buses after eleven."

"I'll call a taxi for you."

"Oh no, you mustn't do that."

"I'll pay for it," she insisted.

I studied the menu. "Just read the left column, don't
look at the right," she said. I laughed sheepishly; she'd
read my thoughts. Still, I chose what cost least. A sponge
cake, eight yuan. A bottle of Coke, three yuan. The
whole bill came to thirteen yuan, one-seventh of my
month's pay. I had to save face. Bracing myself, I took out
fifty yuan.

Young Liang rapped the table and glared at me. "They
only take foreign exchange certificates here." Had she
taken a liking to me?

A man loses face completely if he lets a woman pay for
him. If he were married to a woman like this, he could

never have any self-respect or blow off steam as a husband. It wouldn't do.

Yesterday, on night duty, busy with an emergency
case, I'd hardly slept a wink. And today I'd been on duty
till twelve. I fell asleep as soon as I got into the taxi. At
once I dreamed of my patient the night before, dreamed
his blood pressure was down to zero and his ECG showed
a straight line. I woke with a start.

Although it was only a dream, instead of going home I
asked the driver to take me to the hospital. There I rushed
straight to my ward. The patient was sound asleep. I
heaved a sigh of relief, then made a round of the other
wards to check that all was well before I left. Since I
wasn't on night duty there'd be no bed for me there. It
was so late, where could I go? I decided to look for Xiao
Zao in the high blood pressure research room; his bed
was usually unoccupied.

I walked through the quiet hospital. Each floor was
bisected by a corridor from which jutted consulting
rooms, offices, labs, wards and blood banks . . . like the
skeleton of a flatfish.

In the fifth-floor corridor I met the Spirit of Death. Her
hair was floating over her lovely dark shoulders. Her long
white skirt swept silently over the floor, and underneath
she was wearing a flesh-colored nylon skirt with fancy
borders which must have cost fifteen yuan. She softly
opened the door of each ward to see if anyone needed
carrying off. Today she looked quite placid, my old
friend. Yes, we are old friends. So far neither of us has
won out or lost out.

Xiao Zao, as I had expected, was still up. He was
giving a white mouse its eighth drink of milk. "Shh!" he

whispered. Female mice are afraid of loud noises; high
decibels can drive them out of their minds and make them
eat up their whole litter.

Imagine rats being fussier than men. We put up with a
lot more than high decibels.

I was just going to sleep, when a mouse started giving
birth. Xiao Zao made haste to deliver the little mice and
told me to clean their cage. His concentration on his job
and the way he capered about made him seem like a papa
mouse with a doctoral degree.

"This is the technician's job, you should save your time
for research work," I remarked.

"That's like saying summer's hot and winter's cold, if
you don't eat you get hungry, if you don't drink you get
thirsty, birds fly in the air, fish swim in water, grain coupons and oil coupons are needed to buy grain and oil."

1·12·19—

Professor Hodgkins told me he'd like to visit my house. I
have no house, only a cubbyhole, eight square meters. I
asked the hospital to lend me two rooms and some furniture as props. I signed a guarantee to return them all in
three hours and pay rent for each hour. I was told, "You're
out of date. Now we have an open-door policy; you don't
need to borrow props." Maybe they were afraid I'd borrow those rooms and not give them up. Nowadays some
people go back on their word.

So I went on worrying. I wasn't afraid of Professor
Hodgkins's laughing at my poverty; I was afraid he'd
think the Chinese Communist Party's policy toward intellectuals was simply empty talk. And that would damage our Party's and our country's prestige.

I tried for some days to think of a way to disguise my eight square meters, so as not to give a bad impression of our Party and state. I drew up several plans for rearranging my bed, table and chair and the books piled by the wall, to make the eight square meters appear larger. So that at least I could move in another chair. Or should I borrow a few shrouds from the ward to drape over everything? Planning this was harder than a tricky operation. I racked my brain till my head ached and I couldn't sleep at night. Finally I hit on a way to get two rooms. One room eighteen square meters, the other twenty. Since many on our staff were in desperate need of housing, the hospital had decided to vacate two rooms, one that was eighteen square meters and the other twenty. All I needed was eighteen square meters. I reported this idea of mine to the Party secretary. The pouch under his right eye twitched and made him blink. Pressing one finger under his eye, he said to me, "You go back first."

Go back where? To my eight-square-meter room or to one of eighteen or twenty square meters? He hadn't specified. I paced up and down outside his office, not knowing where to go.

1·16·19—
Professor Hodgkins has brought me several hundred tubes for cardiac intubation, and some silica gel tubes. Some are brand-new, some have been used once. He's really a good old fellow who understands us and our situation. We have no money but we need such tubes badly.

When I studied in San Francisco, I always stayed behind to clean up the operating room after each operation.

The Americans threw away needles, cardiac tubes and silica gel tubes after using them just once. What a waste. After sterilization they could be used again. By the time I came home I'd collected several hundred, which lasted our hospital quite a while.

I know it's a safer way of avoiding infection to throw out used equipment. But a cardiac tube costs more than a hundred dollars. And we don't make them in China. (I don't see why not, since we can make sputniks and rockets. And it should be much easier than that.) And our hospital doesn't have much foreign currency. All hospitals here sterilize these tubes and use them again. Again and again. Until they're worn out. Once when Dr. Zhang was examining a patient, the tube he was using broke off in the vein because it was worn out; he had to cut open the vein to extricate it.

Two days ago Professor Hodgkins started demonstrating different operations. He'd brought his own instruments and apparatus, even his own gown, apron, cap, trousers and shoes—all made of paper. After wearing them once he burned them; that's much safer than sterilizing and reusing them.

He said, "This 'extravagance' is necessary to avoid infecting patients or even causing their death."

Still, I couldn't help rushing to retrieve the appliances he scrapped. The sight of them made me shiver, made my teeth chatter, just like Pavlov's drooling dog. If I ever marry, I doubt that I'll love my wife half as much as those bloody instruments. I held them up like newly killed eels or fragrant, freshly cut melons. I felt as if I were walking on air. Cried out in delight. Turned three somersaults on the floor. I slapped people's cheeks with those trophies, thrust them down their throats . . . spattered blood all over them.

Pay no attention to this nonsense I'm talking; it's simply hallucination.

>< 6

As far as your academic career is concerned, your parents may have lacked forethought. They should have sent you from the start to a model kindergarten, from which you could have gone on to a first-rate middle school. And it didn't occur to them, or maybe they couldn't afford it, to engage a tutor for you while you were in lower middle school to supplement what you were taught there. So you flunked the college entrance exam and became unemployed. No, here we call it "waiting for employment." You were waiting for employment. You might not be too bright, but you were a decent youngster who didn't want to steal or sponge on your parents.

The Central Committee's call to expand private enterprise gave you your opening. You traveled all the way from Guangzhou and Shatoujiao to Beijing, Lanzhou and Sian selling jeans, cheap Hong Kong cosmetics and patent-leather boots. You started off in a small way and found yourself rich overnight. Could easily afford to buy your future in-laws ten catties of crabs costing twenty-five yuan a catty. Your future in-laws' eyes crinkled into slits like crescent moons. They only wished they could marry you themselves. You felt really good! But on your next trip, like a fool, you made the mistake of laying out all your capital and interest. Not realizing that thousands of other people were now in the same line of business.

You didn't realize either that jeans and T-shirts were no longer the rage. To make matters worse, tons of highly profitable clothes were being shipped in duty-free from Japan—it hadn't occurred to our customs that such things would be imported—clothes stripped from the dead or picked out of garbage heaps. These, although secondhand, were smarter than those from the street markets in Shatoujiao.

That busted you. Busted you completely. You were unemployed again. No, again waiting for employment. But you had to put on a bold face for your pals, your future wife and in-laws. When your future wife and in-laws dropped out of sight and your friends cold-shouldered you, you still had to put on a bold face.

Finally, though, you reached the end of your tether. What could you do?

If you persisted in smiling, smiling a warm, sincere, enthusiastic smile, a modest, respectful, approving, admiring smile, the muscles of your face started aching and twitching. Finally the left side of your face, including your left eyebrow, left eye and left corner of your mouth, twisted up. And nothing would cure this contortion, not hot compresses, acupuncture or applications of eel blood. You longed to find a place where your facial muscles could rest.

SUPPOSE your wife had died last year of carbon monoxide poisoning, and you were afraid to light a coal stove again. But your small room faces north and gets no sunshine, so that hunched up with cold you start having heart trouble. And you've got no money to go through the back door, you can only write applications for new housing. You've written enough now to paper a whole room. But you're better off than others; there are plenty worse off than you. Don't you know that? Newlyweds without a room can make love only on some bench in a park; they take along their marriage certificate to prove to the police that they are lawfully wedded. Even such senior scholars as X, an expert on English literature, and Y, an expert on American literature, haven't benefited yet from the policy of improving the conditions of intellectuals. They still live in leaky, drafty, ramshackle rooms. And who are you? What have you done for the country? How can you compare with them? Go to the back of the line.

You have to be an official to get housing. Experts and scholars don't count. Once you make it to assistant bureau head you'll be given an apartment, a car, a telephone and higher pay. That's why in some organizations they have six department heads in charge of one clerk. But a dolt like you can never hope for a post that will bring you housing. All leading positions in your unit, big and small, have been occupied by others who are dividing the loot.

Or why not imitate Hans Christian Andersen's little match girl and strike matches to warm yourself? You won't. That was a fairy tale for children.

You're cold. Put on your quilted vest, quilted coat, trousers and shoes. Put on your cap and scarf, oh yes, and a gauze mask. As if you were an explorer at the South Pole. But you're still cold—what can you do?

SUPPOSE the head of the Personnel Department happened to be your good friend and told you that in view of your qualifications you were going to be appointed head of the Foreign Affairs Department. You might already have been trained in leadership at that center in San Francisco.

For instance, how do you give effective leadership?

How do you handle contradictions between different departments?

How do you deal with clients' complaints?

How do you hold effective meetings?

How do you become a good speaker?

How do you assess the work of subordinates?

How do you write summaries?

You come first in all unofficial tests. But up pops a young fellow to occupy the place that should be yours by right. Even though he can't understand simple English like "eggs sunny-side up or down."

You dare not protest, because he's the son of a powerful minister. And if you complained you might even lose your position as assistant department head. You have to accept his appointment cheerfully and do your best to support him, or, strictly speaking, do his work for him. You have to put on armor to hide your jealousy, to hide it from gimlet eyes able to see through steel and from the eyes of those who analyze you or love you. What would happen if you took off your armor and showed how you felt?

SUPPOSE you work single-mindedly for years on a problem as yet unsolved. Like those characters in novels or films who drink ink instead of milk, blunder into telegraph poles or eat rubber instead of pickles. At last, one day you make a sudden breakthrough and become a celebrity at home and abroad. You can straighten up from your microscope or computer to look around. You discover the goodness of the world, the generosity of human beings, including, naturally, women. And how these women love you—especially her! She worships your brilliance, not setting special store by the Nobel Prize you have won. You face up bravely to the contradiction between your career and marriage, a contest in which you must triumph or die for your cause. You marry this woman who, for love of you, has attempted suicide three times by jumping into the river. You'd never known that a woman could melt a man's heart like this. Even when you go abroad you keep her in mind, your heart aching with love for her.

Long live the food allowance!

Your suitcases are packed with instant noodles or hardtack, in addition to your theses. Your academic achievements make your foreign hosts put you up in five-star hotels. But no matter what hotel you are in, the corridors are pervaded by the smell of Chinese instant noodles. You clutch the money saved on meals, your legs shaking as the result of prolonged malnutrition. For the first time in your life you buy a woman's wristwatch. A dainty eighteen-karat gold wristwatch with only four marks on its brown dial, designed for a modern young lady. From its fine chain hangs a small pendant. Whenever she raises her hand that pendant will swing enchantingly from her smooth wrist.

From your second trip abroad you bring back . . .

From your third trip . . .

From your fourth trip . . .

It gets so that the sight of instant noodles makes you want to throw up like a woman with morning sickness.

In the end you discover that she doesn't love you. She is

having a secret affair with a handsome young lover and playing around with various celebrities. She has sucked in your fame and status (a Nobel Prize winner's wife can count as China's First Lady) and is also enjoying the love of a lusty young man. She is surely the happiest woman in the world.

You're already over fifty, the cynosure of all eyes at home and abroad. You can't afford to appear in gossip columns, and you can't say no to her when she's shedding eyedrop-induced tears. If you so much as have diarrhea it gives rise to all sorts of rumors. . . . Not only must you pretend that you know nothing, you must give everyone, including her, the impression that your home is ideally happy. . . . Sometimes you are so sick of this pretense that you contemplate suicide, but for the sake of your work you have to live on. So now what can you do?

SAY you've always played the part of an iron lady, so tough you can eat iron nails. There'll come a time when you can't keep it up and will long to have a good cry. But you can't find anywhere to cry, so what's to be done?

IN a word, when the suppression of all your feelings seems rational and essential yet finally you can't take it anymore and your only way out is to lose your mind, you simply mustn't go mad. You don't need this world, but this world needs you. How could clever people do without idiots like you?

Come, let's go to the bathhouse. That's where you are happiest. Here you can forget your frustration. For a mere sixty fen you can stay as long as you like—as long as the place is open. Let's hope that bathhouses never disappear.

Watched by the attendant, you take off your coat and clothes, revealing your handsome curves or the ugly scars of cesareans or breast operations on your lean, flabby body. They estimate your income from your under-clothes, discounting your overcoat. Because Chinese scholars, even those as poor as Kong Yi Ji,* always wore a long gown as a status symbol.

In these surroundings you can learn to forget the idea that privacy is sacred and unviolable; you can also learn to forget your sense of shame.

Bathhouses may also be good places for sketching nudes without having to hire models.

You open the locker, with its blend of at least a thou-sand women's sweat, and add your own to it. Even a police dog might be flummoxed here, and if he gets it wrong, he might be discharged and served up as a meal. The papers advise hepatitis-B victims to keep away from bathhouses, to avoid spreading infection. Sound enough, but then where can they go for a bath? They can't copy some of the ethnic minorities, who are bathed only on their deathbeds. If they bathe at home, the summer isn't so bad, but what about the winter? Apart from high officials, who has hot water twenty-four hours a day? If not twenty-four hours a day, two hours a week would do.

Then you walk into the bathhouse with its skylight. The steamy room is like an enormous monster with countless heads, arms and legs, countless breasts and sexual organs. A conglomeration even more appalling than spaceships, rockets or hydrogen bombs. If you were to cut off an arm or a sexual organ, another would appear

---

* *Translator's note:* A penniless scholar in one of Lu Xun's stories.

---

in its place at once. Would appear simultaneously. How much time and effort are needed to build a rocket or spaceship. Yet in only a few seconds, millions of parts of the body are produced.

You jockey for a faucet with three or four heads, seven or eight arms and legs, and the water is now icy cold, now scalding hot. On the other side of the bathhouse two men's voices are raised in a quarrel over water. Their voices carry through the porcelain partition, in a flash becoming so amplified that the world is swallowed up in a raging sea of sound. A little boy, maybe brought by his mother to her bathroom, or a little girl taken by her father to his, sets up a wail in tribute to this first lesson in sex education. Piercing as a clarion call to charge, that wail resounds through the storm. . . .

Come on, you can do as you please here, laugh or cry, grind your teeth, defecate or drop your mask. No one will pay the slightest attention to you.

"SHALL we scrub each other's back?" Chen Yaomei jumped. That voice made her suspect she'd come through the wrong door.

The women's bathroom is on the right, the men's on the left. Had she gone through the right door or the left? The right. No, the left. No, the right.

She looked around and saw one shoulder of the speaker. "I've washed my back," she said. She wouldn't dream of letting a stranger touch her. Especially someone with a voice like that.

"Will you scrub mine, then?"

Yaomei felt it was difficult to refuse.

The speaker, a strapping woman, had a back as broad

and solid as a rolling board. Yaomei had to stand on tiptoe to reach her shoulders.

The towel rubbed down that woman's back, rubbed off whole layers of dirt as if a carpet were being rolled up. The roll of dirt was thinner at the sides, thicker in the middle. It dropped lightly down like a tapeworm, although it was different in color. The bubbling stream of water carried it off with coils of hair, empty plastic shampoo packets and soap, sluicing them into the sewers.

What a boon water is.

At last one of the nearby faucets was free. Water was still gushing from it. The city's water level was said to be very low. Yaomei turned off the water. At once someone called, "What are you doing? I want to rinse myself."

"You can turn it on when you're ready."

"I've paid sixty fen, why not let me have a good bath?"

The faucet was turned on again. The hand gripping it seemed to be wringing Yaomei's throat.

Yes, she'd paid sixty fen, better let her have a good bath.

The flowers in the park may wither overnight, as if galloped over by stampeding horses; the newly erected statue at the end of a street may have one of its arms or legs knocked off; the marble floor of a new bookstore, post office or museum may suddenly be spat on. . . . Such vandalism is actually a form of revenge for years and years of frustration. Yaomei understood that.

Besides, turning off a faucet for a while could hardly solve the city's water shortage.

There were only four dozen bathhouses in town. How could they cater to several million people?

Gradually, the idea of scrubbing backs no longer disgusted Yaomei; she began to see the point of it. In any event, today she'd helped one of those millions get rid of the dirt accumulated over at least a month.

Just then, from not far away she heard a husky and haunting melody. A cross between singing and crooning. She searched for its source. The singer was a woman of indeterminate age, whose long hair, newly washed, lay coiled like a snake over her smooth, plump shoulders. Yaomei had never seen such beautiful shoulders. And the woman's waist was as slender as a girl's. Yet her face, which seemed now young, now old, was crisscrossed with fine wrinkles. She was singing raptly to herself.

She was in another world, that was obvious. The earth had split open and she was standing high on the edge of the fault. The wind on the steppe was blowing hotter and hotter, the sun behind her was shining colder and colder.

How had she bored her way out from the loess heaped over her for billions of years?

Yaomei couldn't understand a word she was singing. But she knew this was a song about the subterranean world below the loess.

Yaomei felt herself falling into the fault. Everything around her was murky. Some force was whirling, squeezing, tugging her. After an initial struggle she remained passive. Even enjoyed the comfort of sinking down. Enjoyed it so much that she nearly cried out in fear. She tossed her head to shake off the drops of water on her face, blurring her eyes, till once again she could see those countless heads, arms and legs, countless breasts and sexual organs.

The singer stared at her mysteriously, as if they had some secret understanding. As if she had carried Yaomei off in a dream. What had she done in that dream? She couldn't remember.

Yaomei put on her clothes and left the bathhouse. By the ticket window stood a foreigner with yellow hair and blue eyes. What did he want?

The bus was fearfully crowded. The conductor kept begging, "Who'll vacate a seat for someone with a child?"

Yaomei hung her head so that only the crown of her hat could be seen. Just now that fellow's eyes had swept over her neck and fixed on her breasts.

She trod lightly on him with the tip of her foot. He was tightly buttoned up in his tunic suit; even his collar was buttoned. Still, she could see his flesh pulsating. She trod on him again and tilted the crown of her hat. She could see that roguish look stealing from the corner of his eyes. She cast a sidelong glance at him. This stunt was easily learned from TV shows.

"What's your opinion of the public bathhouses?" she asked.

He sprang up from his seat and moved away, washing his hands of her. Under his breath he muttered, "Crazy, crazy."

A POSTER in the university advertised a lecture on literature. The speaker was the well-known writer Mr. Norman. His topic was "New Trends in World Literature." The organizers were the research students of the Chinese literature department.

Yaomei detested the teaching methods and examination system at the university. This term she'd tried cutting classes, and her exam results had remained the same.

So she could play truant.

She squeezed onto a window ledge from which she could look down on the auditorium. The cream of the Chinese literature department were strutting up and down the aisles as if unable to find seats good enough to accommodate their great talent.

The crème de la crème was one who had won a reputation for his story "A World Full of Thighs." Working for his master's degree, he was also a spare-time writer. He had unreservedly poured all his piddling dreams about girls into that story.

Draped over his shoulders was the blue serge coat he never took off, not even when buying breakfast in the canteen, probably not even when he went to bed. Under one arm he had a copy of *Ulysses*, now all the rage and the best gauge of a writer's caliber, as well as, of course, some letters from foreigners and announcements of literary conferences. He slapped A's chest, chucked B under the chin, pinched C's nose, swore to D that E was a scoundrel, to F that G was a son of a bitch, and to H that K was a bastard. Only then did he sit down in the middle of the front row.

The speaker was introduced by the department head: ". . . Mr. Norman, one of the most brilliant contemporary writers, is leading the new trend in world literature. For students of our department to listen to his lecture and read his works will provide a wonderful source of inspiration. Today our staff and students are most fortunate to have the chance to hear him. . . . So let us welcome Mr. Norman with hearty applause. . . ."

Mr. Norman spoke for two hours on Asses and Roses, after which he invited questions.

His answers were concise if irrelevant. After each reply

he pointed at the questioner down below. "Have I answered your question?"

The questioners could only make a show of both nodding and shaking their heads.

The accent of the overseas Chinese who was interpreting Mr. Norman's answers added color to the pretense of understanding what was gibberish.

"I've got a question." Unlike the other students, Yaomei didn't get down from her perch on the window ledge and run up to the platform. "May I ask you what your motive is in writing?"

The top students at once started sneering.

"Where's *she* from?"

"The physics department."

"What's she doing here? How can she understand?"

"A dilettante!"

"Asking a childish question like that she'll make Mr. Norman laugh at us, lose face for our department."

The interpreter expressed anger on Mr. Norman's behalf. "Sorry, I can't translate a question like that."

"Why not?"

"It's too impolite."

"Is he polite, making fools of everyone?"

The top students started booing Yaomei. The interpreter cast her smiles into the audience as though each one was a meaty bone. . . . "It's not my duty to answer you," she said.

"You can say that, as you're hired to translate by Mr. Norman, not by me. I've no foreign currency for you, and as *renminbi* is worthless you probably wouldn't want it." With that Yaomei repeated her question in English.

The interpreter had never dreamed that this locally

born and bred, countrified-looking girl could speak better English than she could.

If Chinese decide to do something and are given the least chance, they can always succeed.

Five thousand candidates took the TOEFL in that city in 1984, and the three who got perfect scores had taught themselves English. In 1985, fifty thousand candidates took the TOEFL.

Mr. Norman thought for a moment, then said, "I'm this world's god."

Yaomei retorted, "In that case this world must be impotent. . . ."

The interpreter threw down her glass of tea. The department head, not knowing English, couldn't understand what was up.

Mr. Norman decided to be tolerant. "Okay, okay!" he said.

There was a general outcry.

"Hooligan."

"Shameless."

"Make her apologize."

"Throw her out."

The department head finally caught on. "I'm sorry, so sorry," he apologized. "That student is unbalanced."

By now the interpreter had gone on strike. The department head could only throw up his hands and shrug (very much like a foreigner). "We have no common language, too bad."

THE bus had passed the Gold Dragon Hotel.

Soon she'd be home.

Yaomei lived just behind the Gold Dragon Hotel, opposite its row of garbage cans.

As usual a crowd had gathered around the garbage cans, waiting to scavenge the refuse from the hotel which had already been sifted by the staff.

Foreigners are most generous. They throw away old ties; razor blades; half-full jars of instant coffee; ballpoint pens; stationery; white paper with foreign printing on one side, the back of which can be written on or sold for a good price to paper mills; plastic bags; instructions for the use of samples (these make good covers for school books or can be sold to be pulped); plywood painted with advertisements (which can serve as cupboard shelves) . . . An article in a French paper described Chinese women who go to France as "France's fiancées." The Chinese are growing more and more Westernized.

THE Party secretary called Chen Liansheng in for another talk; it lasted two hours.

He started with modernization, then went on to: raising the standard of living; the importance of public health; the development of the economy and its bearing on the raising of living standards; the medical facilities of the city and hospital and the shortage of nurses; the hospital's long-term and short-term plans; the lack of funds to enlarge the outpatient department, operating rooms and wards; the hospital's relations with its affiliated institutions; the discipline of Party members, discipline shown by acting in unison. . . .

Finally the Party secretary said, "Dr. Chen, I hope you'll consider these things. . . . Our construction funds won't be approved till his father gives the green light. As for clearing up the question of his wife's hymen, it's just because he's so confused that I think he should have a chance to increase his knowledge. So I hope you'll take him as a research student."

After leaving the operating table Chen Liansheng had spent a dozen hours in the observation room. He was worn out. He wanted desperately to sleep, to lie straight down on the floor. But he couldn't possibly doze off while the Party secretary was talking to him. Warm drowsiness flooded over him, invading each cell in his body. He struggled feebly against his somnolence, half his mind awake, the other half asleep.

The sleeping part of his mind had a dream. Dreamed that he had changed into a fancy cream cake and been put on a huge cakestand. People were sitting all around this stand. Or so he guessed, not being able to see them. Since he was a cake, of course he ought to be eaten. Especially since he was already on the stand.

The people sitting around seemed to have no arms or legs, no noses, eyes or mouths, only long, thick tongues.

They were politely deferring to each other.

"Help yourself."

"After you."

"Don't stand on ceremony."

Although no one reached out or cut him into slices, Chen Liansheng was aware that he was diminishing. First the cream rose on his head vanished, then the cream trimming and finally the sponge cake.

Their long, thick tongues, soft yet sharp, licked at him persistently, licked him up bit by bit.

This won't do, he thought. He couldn't let himself be eaten up so senselessly. Was this eating? What way was this to eat? In fact, what did "eating" actually mean? No matter how they ate, they'd swallowed him up. Could he help it if they used tongues instead of teeth? He felt confused. The sleeping half of his brain told him, "No." The wakeful part said, "Yes."

The Party secretary was also confused. "Well, Dr. Chen, will you or won't you?"

BY the time he got on the bus, Chen Liansheng was still nodding. By now his whole mind was asleep. And sleeping in a most undignified fashion. His head kept flopping to one side, making the smart young lady beside him raise her eyebrows and shrink back. He began drooling. As the bus jolted along he slobbered on his Western jacket.

His jacket was of good material, well cut. He had picked it up for two pounds in a London flea market. Some people despised him for this. The money earned by lecturing abroad had been spent on equipment and books for the hospital, or on stethoscopes as presents for his colleagues.

"Last stop! Hey, everyone out!" called the conductor.

Chen Liansheng sprang up and blundered forward. "How's the patient? How's the patient?" he demanded.

"What are you talking about?" The conductor glared at him.

He woke up then. He waved one hand in front of his face and got off without a word.

"Off his nut!" The conductor slammed the door shut.

A VISITOR was waiting for him at home. At first he thought the Party secretary had followed him, and he wondered how he could have gotten there so quickly; but he remembered that the Party secretary could get a hospital car.

His wife, not her usual placid self, jumped up from the sofa. "At last! Teacher Li has been waiting for hours."

His wife looked as if she were flunking a test or undergoing reeducation. He was all too familiar with the feeling. The lives of intellectuals were a long series of tests and spells of reeducation. Tests on this or that, reeducation in one way or another.

She said to the visitor, "Have a talk with Old Chen. There's something I have to see to, if you'll excuse me." At once she went into the kitchen.

Chen Liansheng just couldn't blame his wife for her selfishness and incompetence.

"There's no more gas, we need a new cylinder," she called from the kitchen.

Teacher Li, in charge of Yaomei's class, visited often, because Yaomei was a problem student. The teacher's face was therefore familiar to Chen. For a second, though, he didn't recognize her. Once more his brain seemed divided in two. One half took Teacher Li for the Party secretary and vice versa. The other half could tell the two apart. When he recognized the teacher he said, "Excuse me, Teacher Li, I have to fetch another cylinder of gas."

"Go ahead, I'll wait." The teacher was experienced in waging protracted warfare.

The old fellow in charge of gas was just locking up. "Why didn't you come earlier?" His face was black. "Can't have this. I've already done two hours' overtime. You all say you're busy, busy. Of course you get paid overtime, but who's going to pay *me*?"

Chen Liansheng looked at his watch: it was nine o'clock. "I'm so sorry. I just now got home."

"Isn't there anyone else in your family?"

"Yes. But . . ." How could he explain that his wife had been tied up with a visitor ready to battle to the death?

The old fellow glanced at him and was touched by his tousled white hair.

He was too kindhearted, this gas man. White-haired old men, maidservants, children, women, he pitied them all. Pitied all who came here for gas. They all looked so exhausted and frantic. He tried to guess this customer's occupation. Was he in a government office? No, in that case he wouldn't leave work so late. Cadres had cushy jobs. Supposed to start work at eight, they didn't have to show up till half past and could sit there in comfort to flip through the papers, sip tea and chat, play cards or chess until the ten-o'clock break. Then in no time it was eleven, when they knocked off and had lunch in the canteen or went home for a meal. The afternoon was the same. At the most they wrote a report or a document a few hundred characters long and made a few telephone calls— that was all. He knew. His son-in-law was a clerk in a government office. Were those few hundred characters and those few telephone calls worth a salary of over a hundred a month? The old man didn't think so. Still, he unlocked the door.

As the door opened, he wondered, "How come I've opened it again?"

The small room reeked of gas, although the valves on all the cylinders were screwed tight. Anyone working here all day would turn black in the face. But where could you find a valve that didn't leak gas, water or oil? There are no such valves in China. Chen knew that all the pipes in his apartment leaked and had to be mended constantly.

Passing Building 2, where the Neighborhood Committee met, Chen saw that the lights were still on and three people were inside talking. He put down his cylinder and went in. "Excuse me, may I use your phone?" he asked.

Since the public telephone had been dismantled, he kept coming here to phone. Came so often that the people here found it difficult to refuse him permission.

He made four calls to different wards to ask after his patients. Each time he was told all was well.

All well. But presently there might be changes for the worse. He gave a sigh of mingled relief and worry. At least he could have supper with an easy mind.

After finishing his calls he expressed his thanks. One old woman quipped, "A chief surgeon like you, why don't they give you a phone?"

He could only chuckle by way of a rejoinder.

He found Teacher Li still sitting at home and reproached himself for having forgotten her. After putting down the gas cylinder he grabbed a towel and sat down to listen to her.

"Been busy recently?"

"Uh-huh." He wiped his left cheek with the towel.

"Is your wife all right?"

"Uh-huh." He wiped his right cheek with the towel.

"I hear you're going abroad. Never mind. If your wife has no one to help her out, she can stay with us and I'll look after her. Don't worry. Don't be polite. She's an invalid. . . ."

By now Chen had mopped his face several times.

After demonstrating her patience, warmheartedness

and concern, the teacher laughed diffidently then came to the point. "It's like this: After the winter holidays we organized discussions among the students about what they'd seen and heard in the holidays at home. Their accounts pointed to the conclusion that there's been a big improvement in the Party's style of work. It was generally recognized that in the past a one-sided way of thinking had exaggerated the faults in our country's advance. Weakened faith in the Party and government had given rise to the longing for a savior—that was absolutely wrong. . . ."

Who had concluded that the Party's style of work had improved so much?

Whose way of thinking was one-sided?

Since no one was the subject of the sentence, this was an ambiguous statement and a restrained one, not criticizing the policy. Chen didn't pay much attention. Simply nodded or shook his head in what he considered the appropriate places.

"During this period Chen Yaomei has raised her political level to some extent. However . . ."

Chen knew this "however" meant that the gist was now coming. He stopped mopping his face and pulled himself together to listen carefully.

Just at this point Yaomei happened to come home. She showed no more surprise at the sight of her teacher than if she had been a blue thermos. "Good evening, Teacher Li." After greeting her politely she sat down on a nearby cot. It didn't occur to Yaomei that her presence might inhibit them.

"What brings you home today?" her father asked, hinting that she should leave the room.

"Why shouldn't I come here?" she retorted laughingly. When it came to an argument he was no match for her. She could see that he didn't really want her to leave, and knowing that he couldn't stand her teacher, she turned on the TV.

Channel 1 had a talk on political economy: "Changing goods into commodities is called selling; changing commodities into goods is called buying. . . ." The speaker wore a gray Western suit. Perhaps a chicken tendon had stuck between his right molars. After every sentence his tongue probed his lower right gums in search of it. How could he fish it out with his tongue? He didn't want to pick his teeth with his fingers in front of a mass audience.

The chicken tendon made him uncomfortable, and also affected his thinking and his delivery.

Yaomei's right molars started aching too. She ran her tongue over her teeth, poking about at random. She wished she had a toothpick as big as a poker and could jump into the TV set to jab hard at the cracks between the lecturer's teeth.

Annoyed that nothing had stuck between her teeth, she stood up to change channels. All eight of them showed the same man.

When she tried Channel 1 again, the speaker had changed. Now there was an impressive and resplendent figure, obviously favored by fortune. Not the sort to be plagued by chicken tendons.

". . . It should be evident that effective steps have been taken to rectify our party's style. Yet some comrades refuse to face facts. Recently the son of the Party secretary of C City was executed. What did these people say? They said, 'The papers haven't identified the body, so maybe a scapegoat was put in his place.' . . ."

"Quite right, it's easy to find a scapegoat," said Ya-omei. She liked commenting on what was said on TV. Either taking up some statement or answering some question in advance—and she never missed the mark. Her off-the-cuff opinions always hit the nail on the head, so that her father couldn't tell whether he should listen to the TV or to her.

Teacher Li kept darting anxious, meaningful glances at Chen.

". . . Who says our party's prestige has slumped? If it had, could we have exercised such an international influence?" the resplendent figure continued.

Yaomei started laughing shrilly. Laughed till her stomach ached. "Who can tell what international influence our party has, if any? No one's gone abroad to find out, so how can they prove it?"

"What way is that to talk, Chen Yaomei? How could the TV lie?" Teacher Li had great respect for that resplendent speaker.

"What do a few lies on TV matter? They can be swallowed, digested and excreted, or follow people when they doze off to sink into oblivion. Do you think they're all that important or able to do great damage? Besides, I never said that he was lying, just that we couldn't be sure he was telling the truth. Because the vast majority of Chinese have no chance to see the world, or even to investigate one foreign country."

"All right, let's change the subject." Teacher Li wasn't used to speaking without preparation or standardized answers.

———

"You raised the subject, I didn't." Yaomei stood up again and went over to the TV set. She pushed the other buttons, saying, "Let's try another channel." Her manner was that of a man touting for a peepshow. "Walk up and have a look: ten cents for a girl in her bath. . . ." She switched through the channels again, but all of them showed the same resplendent figure.

"Go to the kitchen, Yaomei, and see if your mother needs any help," Chen urged his daughter.

"Okay." With a mocking glance at him she went into the kitchen.

"See how it is. Recently her ideas have struck me as rather unsound. For instance . . ."

Yaomei came in again with chopsticks and a dish. "She doesn't need me, and the kitchen's so small I'm only in the way there."

Where wouldn't this girl be in the way, Teacher Li wondered.

Yaomei pulled out a folding table by the wall, and with one foot she yanked out its legs so that it stood steadily in the middle of the floor.

At once this round table almost a meter across appeared to occupy the whole place, which had seemed quite roomy before.

Teacher Li's belly began an embarrassing rumbling. It rumbled so loudly that Chen, sitting opposite, heard it.

She'd cycled a dozen kilometers and it was past her suppertime. She was hungry.

"Do share our simple meal with us, Teacher Li."

"No, no, thank you. I ate before I came."

"You mean lunch?"

"Supper, supper."

Yaomei's lips puckered in a smile, and she didn't insist. She knew the teacher would refuse. Even pressing her mouth to a bowl of rice would be no use.

"Since you've come home, Chen Yaomei, you can listen too. My views may not be correct, but you can consider them."

"If you think they may not be correct, why state them?"

After a second's dismay Teacher Li persevered. "I think the most important thing for you as a student is to study hard, to qualify yourself to make a contribution to society. . . ."

"I get five★ in all subjects."

"Of course that's very good. But can't you do even better?"

She didn't specify how. Unless they started making six the top grade, thought Yaomei.

"Do you still advocate students' burying themselves in the classics, oblivious to the outside world? Don't you think the more people concern themselves with state affairs, the better it is for the nation? Don't you think it is the duty of a good citizen to watch out for poverty, injustice, malpractice, bribery and corruption, and to battle to the end against all abuses? Chairman Mao urged us to pay attention to great affairs of state. You can't negate all his teachings just because he had his faults. We can't be such pragmatists."

"The Party and the government will attend to such things. Are we greater than the Party? More enlightened?

★ *Translator's note:* The highest grade.

More correct? More capable? That brings us back to your old problem: Don't set yourself up as a savior. You're still young, Chen Yaomei, and politically immature. Be careful you don't make mistakes. Once you've made a political mistake you can never succeed in life. This is what I came to discuss with your father, out of concern for your political progress."

Such talk sounded so familiar; Chen Liansheng felt he had heard it all before.

He cast his mind back several decades to the eve of Liberation, when he had joined his college underground. Their dean had harped on the same theme: "The duty of students is to study hard. The country's affairs can be left to the government. They're not your business!"

He had lost faith in his own judgment. His brain seemed split again into two halves engaged in an endless dispute.

He thought it strange the way every time Teacher Li came she held forth nonstop. Surely there was a limit to what could be said on any single subject. Chairman Mao's selected works came to only five volumes, Lenin's to only four, the complete works of Marx and Engels to only fifty.

"Did you want to tell my father about Mr. Norman's lecture?" asked Yaomei. "I've already told him."

"That's good, then." Her teacher turned to Chen. "What's your opinion?"

"I don't think it's important. Foreigners are forever running us down, yet some of us are afraid even to fart. Do you listen to foreign broadcasts? You should. They make such a point of pulling us to pieces, what does it matter if we criticize them? Yaomei's views don't represent the Party or the state. How can a nonentity like her affect our foreign relations?"

Teacher Li could hardly believe that it was a Communist talking. But Chen Yaomei's dossier stated that her father was a Party member.

The policy of opening up meant opening up the economy, not ideology. Talk of opening up didn't mean that there were no restrictions, that all bans could be lifted. It was because of the widespread misunderstanding about this that so many wrong trends had surfaced. And these were reflected inevitably in the university. Living in a family like this, how could Chen Yaomei help being politically muddled.

Teacher Li rated high in institutions of higher learning as a model teacher, one of the most progressive. She hadn't achieved this by sucking up to superiors, trimming her sails to the wind or talking sweetly while trampling on decent people. She'd achieved it by hard work. She'd come to the Chens' place at least five times, for instance, cycling all the way from the southeast corner of town to the northwest. For a woman of nearly fifty, it was hard if the weather turned windy or rainy. Often she'd nearly been knocked down by a bus. Even if you observed the traffic regulations, sooner or later you'd be involved in a crash.

Or take today: Her stomach was rumbling, she was faint with hunger. By the time she left, the restaurants and groceries would have closed. She wouldn't be able to buy so much as a bun. "Changing commodities into goods is called buying." She'd have to cycle right across town again. She'd love to have supper here. Steamed bread with scallions, shredded meat fried with pickles, noodles with egg soup . . . it was all laid out on the table. But if she touched a bite, what would become of her reputation as "incorruptible"?

She knew quite well that the students didn't respect her. They simply humored her, saying what she wanted to hear. Because if the comments on their graduation certificates were unfavorable, they'd never get a good job or be promoted, much less be able to join the Party or go abroad. They'd have to go where conditions were toughest. There weren't many like Chen Yaomei, who didn't despise her but was always arguing with her. Although there was pity mixed with her respect.

Ah, how hard it was to make a reputation for oneself as progressive.

But this was the only way for a teacher with no special qualifications to hope to get ahead. She'd never make it to associate professor, let alone professor. How many people like her were there in all China? After all, there was only one professor of moral education in the whole country.

If she didn't go all-out in this way, she'd be no better off than her younger brother, who taught middle school. During the winter and summer holidays he went to the station with a pedicab to pick up fares and luggage. Or sold dumplings in the free market. "Changing goods into commodities, that's selling." Even in his dreams he'd call out, "Come and buy 'em, come and buy 'em, pork and cabbage dumplings, piping hot!" He used to wake up the whole family. Set them all worrying about his dumplings. Had he put in too much baking powder? Or too little? How could they go on like this, year in, year out?

Once her brother's stall was next to that of one of his

former students. The student said to him, "Teacher, in school you kept criticizing me and warning me that if I didn't work hard, I wouldn't get into college. But now aren't you selling dumplings here with me?"

Such was the fate of a Chinese intellectual!

THE young carpenter called in a gang of his cronies to beat up Hou Yufeng again. After this beating Hou went for emergency treatment and had an X ray taken. Three of his right ribs were broken. The doctor on duty sent him straight to the surgery department.

"Bones take a hundred days to heal." Hou Yufeng figured it out. This meant he could spend three months in the hospital. Could have a good rest for three months. It occurred to him that it would have been more advantageous to break one rib at a time. Three times three was nine. Then he could have had a good rest for nine months. Still, three months wasn't bad either.

Word came that the carpenter had been detained by the police for half a month for inciting others to brawl. It would have been better, Hou thought, if the police had waited till his discharge from the hospital to detain the carpenter. Then he could have had another couple of weeks' good sleep.

Translated by Gladys Yang